Blood Libels

ALSO BY CLIVE SINCLAIR

Bibliosexuality (1973)
Hearts of Gold (1979)
Bedbugs (1982)
The Brothers Singer (1983)

BLOOD LIBELS

Clive Sinclair

Farrar · Straus · Giroux

NEW YORK

First published in Great Britain by Allison & Busby Limited, 1985
First American edition, 1986
Printed in the United States of America
First printing, 1986

Library of Congress Cataloging-in-Publication Data
Sinclair, Clive.
   Blood libels.
   I. Title.
PR6069.I52B5   1986   823'.914   86-2036

Sections of this novel first appeared, in somewhat different form,
in *London Tales, Encounter* and *The Jewish Quarterly*.
The author also wishes to acknowledge the assistance of
the Arts Council of Great Britain.

For Fran and Seth

I Scriptophobia

1

Insomnia is my inheritance, though I would have preferred amnesia. My mother, a pessimist cursed with second sight, was so terrified of her prophetic dreams that she became addicted to a well-known brand of slimming tablets with anti-soporific side-effects. My father, the optimist, was corpulent despite his peptic ulcer. Being an optimist, he secretly devoured late-night snacks of smoked salmon and dill on rye or toasted Jarlsberg with avocado, smuggled in from the local deli, which inevitably caused nocturnal indigestion, the enemy of sleep. To this day I cannot bear silence after dark (not a problem of late), a legacy of those long early-morning hours when, at any given moment, my anorexic mother or my dyspeptic father would be wandering about the house in search of unobtainable comfort.

Having become a nocturnal predator with nothing to prey upon but my own memories, I have been killing time by reliving the past, with a view to understanding the present catastrophe. And the more I chew over those events, the more it seems to me that the holistic approach to history, which sees it as the synthesis of impersonal forces, is completely wrong-headed.

My last history teacher thought it fitting to mock those fossilized anti-determinists from east of Berlin, who maintained that had the Queen of the Nile's nose been of a less sublime shape Mark Antony would never have fought the Battle of Actium and thereby lost the world. A most naïve analysis, we were assured by our teacher, a man who held that history was a science studied by artists. History could never be a picturesque chapter of accidents, he continued confidently, because there is no such thing as an accident. An accident is merely the coincidence of unexpected factors which, once explained, quickly become part of the causal chain. Those who persist in stressing the importance of chance in history tend to be its victims, he made clear, or losers like Trotsky, who claimed in mitigation that the "historical law is realized through the natural selection of accidents".

I remember, also, a simple diagram our hermaphrodite science master drew on the blackboard to demonstrate how heat is conducted along a metal bar. Being the sports coach as well in his masculine periods, he chalked up eleven pin men in a line, representing molecules, the first with a ball at his feet. Since heat moves from hot to cold, he explained, the chain reaction is activated by applying a flame to one end, the extra energy causing the stationary molecules to vibrate and thus pass the ball along the line.

The history teacher must have seen cause and effect linked in much the same way, for his was a closed world, like the school itself, where everything was determined by a higher authority, be it the headmaster, Nature, God or the iron laws of economics and physics. In such a universe there was no space for any deviations, such as Cleopatra's beauty or Rabbi Nathan's lust.

I am convinced that if Rabbi Nathan hadn't tried to rape Helga, our German au pair, during the course of my bar-mitzvah celebrations at the Café Royal on the evening of 21 May 1961, things would have turned out very differently. No need to tell you what I mean by "things". I am well aware that it is possible to find more obvious reasons for what happened — only a fool could fail to see the symbolic potential of an unpopular and unattractive and *Jewish* Chancellor of the Exchequer presiding over mass unemployment — but I would remind you of Raymond Aron's distinction between "immediate causes" and "remote origins". I shall leave the "remote origins" to others. Here are the "immediate causes".

A few may recall that *Rabbi Nathan's Folly* (Potemkin Press, 1973) was the title of my first novel; fewer still will have read it. For those who have not — nearly everyone — I feel an obligation to begin with a digest of that unfortunate book, not out of misplaced pride, I assure you, but only because what began life as literature has now become a fact of history, or so I believe. When Princip fired his gun at Sarajevo the bullets killed millions, for assassinations, though accidental, are planned with consequences in mind. Rabbi Nathan's crime was exactly the opposite, since it was committed in the expectation that it would remain secret and inconsequential; and so it would have done, had I not grown up to be a writer.

2

In his heyday Rabbi Nathan made Jeremiah the Prophet seem a forgiving sort. No one was spared his righteousness, least of all those families with a son approaching his bar mitzvah. God help any boy whose Saturday morning attendances were not regular enough! Come the day, he will be standing in the front row of the synagogue, his newly broken voice still resounding in his ears, while our firebrand of a rabbi denounces his parents for failing to bring him up as a worthy member of the House of Israel. To spare ourselves this public humiliation, the Silkstones appeared in shul every Saturday morning during my twelfth year, leaving Helga at home to prepare the shabbas meal.

And what meals awaited us upon our return! Helga would emerge from the kitchen, clasping a tureen of pungent soup, liquid gold which she ladled into our porcelain bowls, the aroma of the broth mingling poignantly with her perfumes, natural and man-made. She ate with us, though she didn't remove her apron, which stopped abruptly beneath her breasts, as if they weren't prominent enough already. My parents were not blind to such things, of course, but what could they say? Helga's bosom, because unmentionable, became an object of fascination, my promised land; her taut jumper taunted me like an obscure riddle — I could look without really seeing the fullness thereof. No less tender were her slices of veal in a sauce of artificial cream.

Suspicious of the white meat, my mother said, "You're sure this is veal?"

"It's from Leslie Mann," replied Helga, "one hundred per cent kosher."

Her chicken was a miracle; roasted in honey and stuffed with chestnuts, it had us clucking with pleasure. Her steaks were not for the unsanguine, until she explained that the juices were a mixture of burgundy and ketchup. Her new potatoes resembled polished pebbles, yet tasted like butter. My mother had surrendered her oven uneasily, reminding Helga always to light the gas rings immediately, but even she had to admit that we were eating better than ever before.

"Where did you learn to cook so beautifully?" she asked.

"At home," replied Helga. "Mamma was a caterer."

The aforementioned relative sent a chill through us all, being a reminder that Helga was not an isolated phenomenon, but the offspring of a woman whose recent activities we dared not question.

Let us consider that word "recent". As far as I am concerned, Beatlemania, President Kennedy's assassination and the Six-Day War are recent events, yet they are actually more distant today than was the Second World War in 1960, which was prehistoric even then. In short, one's view of history tends to be egocentric: I remember where I was on 22 November 1963 (listening to the radio in my bedroom) and on 5 June 1967 (being examined by a doctor at the headquarters of the Jewish Agency — blood pressure, on the high side of normal; urine, none available — to determine whether I would stand up as a replacement kibbutznik), but on 8 May 1945 I was still on deposit in the genetic bank. As a matter of fact my parents did not make the withdrawal (by not making the withdrawal, if you see what I mean) for another three years, and it was not until Friday, 14 May 1948, that I was able to emulate the great Houdini, or so I have been led to believe.

There was a double celebration in the synagogue on the following morning for, by coincidence, it had come to pass

Scriptophobia

at midnight as the Mandate ran out in Palestine that my father's erstwhile acquaintance, David Ben-Gurion, had proclaimed the birth of *Medinat Yisrael*, the State of Israel, at a hall in Tel Aviv.

Of course I was not able to attend the service in person, being on my mother's breast at the time, but I know the legend well enough of how Rabbi Nathan pointed to my father from the pulpit and cried out: "David Silkstone, your boy is chosen even among the chosen. It is the greatest of mitzvahs to be born on the same day as the Jewish state. It is a mitzvah that you cannot ignore. You must name your son after Jacob the patriarch to whom the Lord spoke, as it is written: 'I am the Lord, the God of your father Abraham and the God of Isaac; the ground on which you are lying I will give to you and your offspring. Your descendants shall be as the dust of the earth; you shall spread out to the west and to the east, to the north and to the south. All the families of the earth shall bless themselves by you and your descendants. Remember, I am with you: I will protect you wherever you go and will bring you back to this land. I will not leave you until I have done what I have promised you.' Little Jacob's birth on the day of days is proof positive that the promise has been redeemed. *Am yisrael chai*. The people of Israel live!"

At which, so I am told, the entire congregation shouted out my Hebrew name, Yakov ben David! So Jacob it was, amended variously to Jakie or Jake.

My conclusion is that in order to understand the world you inhabit it is necessary to step outside of yourself. Failure to do this will lead first to solipsism and thence to madness, as you come to believe that your insignificant corpus is actually the terrestrial body politic. Thus I am able to understand why my mother attempted to disguise Helga's nationality by ostentatiously praising the cleanliness of the Swiss whenever we had visitors lest, God forbid, Rabbi Nathan should learn that we were sheltering a daughter of Germany beneath our roof, but not why she employed her in the first place.

11

Blood Libels

There was no religious injunction against German au pairs of course, even in 1960, but that wouldn't have appeased Rabbi Nathan, who regularly departed from his prepared sermon in order to denounce those members of the synagogue who had just acquired Mercedes cars. God knows how, but he always knew their names. Poor Messrs Bloom, Meyer and Cowan — those over-conspicuous consumers — blushed with shame or anger, while the righteous tut-tutted.

"But even worse than them," Rabbi Nathan's large head oscillated, causing his spade-like beard to quiver, "is the fond foolish father, blessed with wealth, who cannot wait for his son's seventeenth birthday so that he can present him with a brand new Volkswagen. Has he forgotten so quickly the name of their instigator? In time we may forgive — though not in our lifetime — but we must never forget. Never! Never!"

If you ask me, Rabbi Nathan was autophobic, hating especially the cars driven illicitly to his Saturday service by those members of his congregation who didn't fancy the walk, for Rabbi Nathan believed, above all, in the sanctity of the sabbath.

"The man who does not keep the sabbath holy is no Jew, just as a woman who beats her child is no mother," he declared on the last Saturday of August 1960. "Nothing is determined by biology — as we above all peoples should know — but by the heart. If your heart is not in it, neither are you. Many of you, I know, will be running to football matches this afternoon, making a mockery of your presence here. To them I say, leave now. You are no Jews. Your religion is football!"

My father fidgeted in his seat, as if in half a mind to obey his rabbi's command, for he more than most was looking forward to the first home match of the season, soccer being his great passion, giving him the opportunity to relive his finest hour.

3

Now here's some real history for you. An eyewitness account of the creation of Wingate Football Club, as told to me by David Silkstone, one of the founding fathers. It happened in that year of miracles, 1948, though its origins were earlier still.

There is no record of any of my ancestors, neither maternal nor paternal, ever having fought in a war before September 1939. The nearest anyone came, so far as is known, was my father's father, who was actually photographed in the Tsar's uniform, before he changed his mind and fled Russia with his wife in 1905. My father, therefore, blessed with this pacific heritage, had little idea what to expect when he entered the Royal Artillery training camp at Sidcup and became Private Silkstone 1604440. He was, in fact, a volunteer, believing he had a duty to show Englishmen of longer standing that Jews were prepared to do more than shit in their pants at the sight of a Nazi.

"First they taught me how to shoot," he said. "Believe me, Jacob, it is a very peculiar sensation to see a man through the foresight of a rifle and know that you have his future in your hands. A squeeze of the trigger and all his worries and hopes will be nothing but a mockery. I prayed that I would never have to fire anything except blanks. I did not like doing God's work."

His prayer was not answered. On the contrary, he was moved to bigger things, the heavy ack-acks, whose 4.5-inch shells were supposed to make the Luftwaffe think twice about bombing London. Every day for a month he was part of a nine-man gun detachment that fired empty shells at the sleeves of target planes, hoping to draw blood from the invisible arms they contained. Nothing was real, not even the war in those early days, only the haemorrhoids that came from sitting for hours on the iron seat when it was your turn to spin the wheel that elevated the giant barrels.

"But even more irritating than the piles, as far as I was

13

concerned," said my father, "was the genteel anti-Semitism of the English officers."

The anti-Semitism among his fellow gunners was cruder, but at least it could be answered. The last word was available to all. It was at its worst when the training was at an end and there was nothing the enlisted men could do except fight among themselves, the real enemy having not yet overrun France. At which point my father, not a keen boxer, had an inspiration.

He approached the 56th Heavy Anti-Aircraft Brigade's new commanding officer, Captain Orde Wingate, sent to Sidcup as a punishment for philo-Semitism, and suggested that the soldiers be formed into football teams in order to absorb the aggressive tendencies the training had created.

"Certain natural divisions have already appeared among the men, sir," said my father, "so much so that I now mix only with Jews. There are more than enough of us to form a team."

"You shall be known as the Maccabees," said Wingate, who, some believe, developed his famous theory of long-range penetration as a result of studying the devastating effect of my father's pin-point passes, from deep in his own half, upon the opposing team's defence.

"Our plan of action was simple," said my father, "to push the ball up as quickly and as accurately as possible, either from the centre or the wings, to give our forwards a chance at goal before their defenders had an opportunity to regroup."

The strategy worked, and by May 1940 the Maccabees had defeated teams representing England, Ireland, Scotland, Wales, the Colonies and Dominions (excepting India), India and Free France, on the way to the final where they played the only other unbeaten side, picked from the growing number of Polish and Czech exiles, for the Anti-Nazi Trophy.

"It was a hard game," said my father, "the hardest, because we both had something to prove. Well, I suppose we must have had more, because we won, would you

Scriptophobia

believe, with a goal in injury time. That's an afternoon I won't forget in a hurry. They scored first, the result of a mix-up in our defence but, thank God, we managed to equalize. Then, with a few moments to go, their outside-right put over a cross that found the centre-forward — a man with a kick like a mule — with only our goalie to beat. The shot went one way, he went the other, and we knew we'd lost. But a miracle happened. Somehow our goalkeeper — I wish I could remember his name — managed to change direction mid-flight and just tipped the ball over. The corner kick was meant for their centre-half, the size of an ox, but it ended up at my feet instead, so I booted it as hard as I could in the direction of their goal. As luck would have it, the ball bounced just right for our little inside-left, who beat one man, then another, before tapping it over their goalie's head and walking it into the empty net. Everyone went crazy, including our erstwhile detractors.

"We proved something all right that day, Jakie. Wingate's wife presented the trophy, a pewter tankard, and Wingate himself made a speech. 'After two thousand years the Jews have awakened,' he said. 'I have witnessed the results in Palestine, and again today at Sidcup. Our leaders believe that, in their hour of mortal danger, the French will rediscover moral resources, not seen since Napoleon, and defeat the Germans. But they are fooling themselves. France will fall and Britain will stand alone — at least until the day when America and Russia decide to come off the sidelines. But I tell you all that this need not be so. For we have at our disposal the most powerful ally any nation could desire: God's chosen people, the Jews. With them on our side we will have not peace but victory with honour, for their righteousness will be with us as we cast the burden of guilt for this unholy war from our shoulders. And that is why we will be triumphant, because we owe freedom to the Poles, the Czechs and, above all, the Jews. I swear to you here today that I shall go to Whitehall from this place to insist upon the formation of a Jewish

Brigade, which I personally will lead to Berlin.' By now he had probably forgotten what the tankard was for, but he gave it to me anyway with these words, 'The Lord is with thee, thou mighty man of valour.' "

My father laughed bitterly, rubbing his distended belly. "He should see me now."

4

But in September 1940 my father was a real soldier, one of the defenders of Bomb Alley, the southern approach to London. By then he had risen to the rank of gun sergeant and was in command of an anti-aircraft battery. Night after night he stood upon the gun sites of Sidcup, a grim fortune-teller, reading destinies in his range-finder and his predictor, and yelling: "Two degrees west!" or: "Ten degrees north!" so that wheels turned and the guns stood ready in silent anticipation. Meanwhile the shadowy fuse-setters and loaders were doing their midnight chores, shouting as they progressed, "Shell primed! Breach opened! Ready for firing!" And my father would hold his breath, for fear of disturbing some magical equilibrium, before ordering, "Fire!" Smoke and sparks and the jitterbugging barrels were a prelude to a spotlit *pas de deux* occasionally so perfect in execution that it seemed to require a new law of physics to describe properly. Only when my father saw the plane descend in its last dizzy, dazzling dance did he remember that there were men inside. Even so, it took quite an effort not to enjoy killing them.

One evening, late that same month, Wingate suddenly appeared at the door of my father's Nissen hut and said, "Sergeant Silkstone, get ready. We're going to London."

A chauffeur drove them from Sidcup to Hampstead despite the fact that they would be arriving after dark, when the bombing would probably be at its worst. This didn't worry Wingate, of course, whose mind was elsewhere, though something was making him tense, my father could see that.

Scriptophobia

"I have not forgotten the promise I made to you on the playing fields of Sidcup," he said, "but no one will listen to me, not even your own people. Tonight you will see for yourself the truth of my words." That was all, until he instructed his driver to stop outside a house near the Heath.

"Come, Sergeant Silkstone," said Wingate.

My father followed and stood rigidly, as if at attention, while they waited for someone to open the door.

"Can you guess who it was?" asked my father, the first time he told me the story. I couldn't, of course. "Well," he said triumphantly, "it was Ben-Gurion."

Flicking through a book about Ben-Gurion recently, I found a photograph of him taken in 1918 when he was a soldier in the Jewish Legion. I swear that when I first saw it I thought it was of my father, so similar were they in their army uniforms. I wonder if Ben-Gurion noticed the resemblance when he said, "*Shalom*, Orde, and welcome to your friend."

Instead of inviting them in he chose, inexplicably, to return with them to the car. So they drove around Hampstead in darkness, discussing the problems of forming a Jewish Brigade, while enemy planes flew overhead and houses, giving a huge grunt, as if relieved at being able to surrender to gravity at last, blazed up out of the darkness.

"I have brought Sergeant Silkstone along," said Wingate, "because he has already proved beyond doubt that Jewish soldiers, when fighting for each other, have it in themselves to be invincible."

"How was this?" asked Ben-Gurion.

So Wingate recalled the short but glorious history of the Maccabees, as if it were indeed another chapter of the book of books.

"You have beaten the English at their own game," said Ben-Gurion, obviously no devotee of soccer, "you are to be congratulated."

"Now it is your turn," said Wingate. "I beg you to call for

17

volunteers to join a Jewish Brigade. Don't wait for permission from the British."

"It would not be diplomatic," said Ben-Gurion.

"Diplomacy is an English speciality," snapped Wingate, losing his temper. "They will run rings around you."

"In that case," said Ben-Gurion, "I must follow the example of your friend."

"I fear that you lack his passion," said Wingate.

Ben-Gurion's face expressed his anger so precisely that no words were needed, nor were any offered. Wingate too stayed grimly quiet. My father, squeezed between these men of destiny on the worn leather of the car's back seat, knew that history itself was a fellow traveller and felt as if his sole function was to be its faithful scribe, but he could not, for the life of him, grasp the significance of the journey, which would certainly have ended in silence were it not for the fact that Ben-Gurion's lodgings had been hit by a bomb in his absence.

"A man does not escape the Angel of Death for no reason," said Wingate. "My dear friend, you have been spared to do great deeds."

The way I see it is this: if my father hadn't made the Maccabees into such a success there would have been no Proclamation on 14 May 1948, not by Ben-Gurion at any rate. Other historians regard it differently, of course; indeed, most omit my father's name from the passenger list on that fateful night, which shows you how much they know.

As it turned out, the Jewish Brigade was not established until 1944, some six months after Wingate's death in Burma. Another nine months and the war itself was over, the Jewish Brigade disbanded and my father demobbed. He kept in touch with a few of his former team-mates and, every other Saturday, they met amid the green acres of Sunnyhill Park to kick a ball about. But the games lacked the competitive edge that had given the Maccabees their spirit, and they became more and more irregular, and would probably have ended altogether if it hadn't been for

the remarkable renaissance of the Badger, as Bruno
Gascoyne was known.

5

Whenever I wanted to annoy my father, as I often did
during my adolescence, I ostentatiously read one of
Gascoyne's books, usually his modern version of Malory, a
classic of the inter-war years and no chore, despite its
unmistakable anti-Semitism. Set not in mythical Camelot
but in Edwardian England, it tells the story of an idealistic
society twice doomed: by the weakness of the flesh, by the
plots of envious outsiders. Thus Morgan le Fay becomes
Fay Morgenthal, an American Jewess; black of hair, eye
and soul. Her son, the dreaded Mort, spies not only upon
adulterous Lance and Jenny, but also upon Britain itself in
the cause of Levantine world domination. There is a
certain poetic justice in this, however, for Mort's natural
father is none other than Art, albeit from a union
concluded long before his marriage to Jenny. Thus,
according to Gascoyne, Britain's tragedy was in part
self-inflicted. Nor did he exclude himself from blame.
Arthur's diminished name reflected upon himself as an
artist, seduced from the Commonwealth by the appeal of
cosmopolitan exotica. Gascoyne's panacea was Heil Hitler
and Hail Mary! He converted to Catholicism and fell in
love with Europe's shining dictators, wishing to supervise
the building of a New Order in Britain, an ambition
scotched by the war and subsequent imprisonment as a
potential traitor.

My father, understandably angered, took me to Trafalgar
Square during the election of 1964 to hear Gascoyne for
myself. Flanked by lions, the failed dictator spoke
passionately about the Empire to the remaining members
of his once mighty British Party. He reminded his listeners
how, at its best, it had "disinterestedly brought civilization to Asiatics and niggers until it was destroyed as a
result of two Jewish wars".

Blood Libels

"Anti-Semite!" cried my father.

Gascoyne paused. "My friend," he began, "now that you have drawn attention to yourself perhaps you will be so good as to assist me in clearing up a little mystery. We have heard *ad nauseam* about the six million martyrs, but very little about any heroes. I have spoken to many soldiers who fought in the King's army, and not one of those sturdy patriots can recall a single Hebrew warrior fighting alongside them. Where were you all? Sucking us dry on the home front, that's where."

"Lies!" yelled my father, but Gascoyne was no longer listening.

It was calumnies like that and worse, uttered when the blood of war was hardly dry, that had persuaded my father and his friends to do something; the something being the establishment of an all-Jewish football club.

"We wanted people to know that not all Jews were walking skeletons or else fat gown manufacturers," said my father, "that Jews could be athletes as well as bankers."

Sad to say, this attempt to hellenize the image of the Jew suffered some early setbacks as their application was rejected in turn by the Isthmian, Athenian, Delphinian and Spartan Leagues, and it was not until August 1948 that they played and lost their first game of senior football in the London League.

Their declared aim was to improve the relationship between Jew and non-Jew, and so seriously did they take it that they did not have a man sent off nor even concede a penalty for well over two seasons. Unfortunately their victories were almost as rare. Such was still the case when I began to watch them in the early fifties, long after family and financial pressure had cut short my father's playing days. Having never heard of Orde Wingate, after whom my father had insisted upon calling the team, I thought the name was some hopeful boast and joked as we trooped home down the Watford Way after yet another home defeat that Losegate would be more accurate — my first recorded attempt at literary effect.

20

6

However, on that autumnal Saturday in August 1960 Wingate unexpectedly beat the league champions in a spectacular match that set its seal upon the whole of that season. By the end of it Wingate were themselves runners-up, and in the final of the league cup, for the first time in their history. But why had they previously been unable to emulate their illustrious predecessors, the Maccabees? The answer is simple: because they were more concerned with being liked than winning. They played for love, for love of the game, for love of their fellow man, and we loved them for it, and so did they, we assumed. Thus it went on — until June of that memorable year, when the new manager arrived, a man well practised in the *realpolitik* of football.

"Of course everyone likes playing against us," he said, "why shouldn't they? They know they're going to win. When we start handing out the beatings we'll see what they're really made of."

And so began the most rigorous training sessions the players had ever experienced, which produced the startling results aforementioned, as well as a satisfying increase in anti-Semitism. The cup-run, in particular, was so nerve-racking that I was usually still quivering when my parents kissed me good night on their way to the theatre or to see friends and left me alone with Helga.

During the course of the evening, as we sat watching the Ultra Bermuda, the thrill of the hard-won victory was transformed almost imperceptibly into the anticipatory excitement of an unbidden hard-on. A normal lad, I suppose, would have excused himself and taken matters into his own hands, but I lacked the self-confidence. I was far too frightened to masturbate alone, though I could never have done it in front of anyone else either. To this day I find great difficulty in fulfilling even the simplest function in public — I still cannot pee in the presence of strangers — but here's the paradox: my actions are meaningless unless they are observed. These days I have (or had) the ideal compromise: I write in private for publication. But then I had no such outlet. So what was I to do? Unlucky Helga soon found out the solution to that.

"I'm going to bed," I would say, at about ten-thirty, and went, but not there. Sometimes I would linger until I heard Helga switch off the television, whereupon I would creep downstairs, stripped to my underpants, and wait for her in the kitchen, where I toyed with our late poodle.

"Sorry," she would say as she came in, echoing the "Sorry" I uttered as I ran out.

Back in my bedroom I examined my Aertex briefs to ascertain exactly how much flesh she had been able to see through the tiny holes.

Or else I would take my pants off altogether and have a bath, leaving the door unlocked and even slightly ajar. Having listened to Helga go up the stairs and into her room I would temporarily vacate the bathroom and loudly close the door to my own room, before sneaking silently back. Then, hearing Helga's footsteps across the landing, I would position myself in such a place that I would be impossible to miss when Helga entered and saw her mistake. Why did I do it? Did I really want her to scream threats at me instead of apologizing, to punish me even? I don't think so. I believe, rightly or wrongly, that what I wanted was for someone, preferably Helga, to acknowledge the existence and function of those unspeakable parts of my body and, more importantly, to take responsibility for them, not pedagogically but literally — after all, I was rapidly approaching manhood, as Mr Mendel kept reminding me.

7

Mr Mendel, the shammus, had been designated to teach me the dozen or so verses of the Torah I was destined to sing at my bar mitzvah. He wore a pin-stripe waistcoat, from a pre-war suit purchased in Warsaw, and took snuff. The box from which he pinched his piquant powder was decorated with an artist's impression of Solomon's temple. Needless to say, my own idea of the extant city of Jerusalem was as unlikely as that artist's. I imagined it suspended midway between heaven and earth, beneath a golden dome, so that when viewed from the city the sky was always shining. But just as I knew that Helga was not actually compatible with my fantasies, so I realized that the divided city of 1960 was nothing like my vision.

Even so, I sensed that I had, in my wild flights, divined something of the essence of person or place; without understanding the process I was, however clumsily, endeavouring to comprehend the incomprehensible — which also sums up my progress in Mr Mendel's lessons. I had, to be sure, studied the aleph-bet at *cheder* — with all the enthusiasm of a Philistine.

"Why do I need to learn Hebrew?" I asked my instructor.

"Because you are a Jew," she replied.

"But all the Jews I know talk English," I protested.

"God doesn't," she replied, "He only listens to Hebrew."

"But I never speak to God," I said, "I don't believe in Him."

Instead of trying to convert me with ontological, cosmological or teleological arguments, the defender of our benevolent deity slapped me around the face. "I'll teach you to say such things," she screamed. True to her word, though ignoring that on the door, she dragged me into the Ladies' lavatory, where she violently washed out my mouth with soap and water. If only Helga could have been so masterful!

It was also Mr Mendel's duty to instruct me in the wearing of *tefilin*.

"We put them on every morning because of what is written in the Pentateuch," he explained. " 'And it shall be for a sign unto thee upon thy hand, and for a memorial between thine eyes, that the law of the Lord may be in thy mouth.' '' He removed two black boxes from a velvet bag and demonstrated how to attach them to the body by means of leather thongs. "We place one upon our left arm to influence the heart," said Mr Mendel, "the other on our forehead, the seat of the mind."

I smiled when I glimpsed my reflection in his hall mirror, for instead of a Jewish juvenile I saw a budding rhinoceros. The small erection on my temple faithfully represented what was going on within. Puberty had ensured that the triangle of connections between heart, mind and tongue was no longer spontaneous, but subject to a series of checks, forcing my censored thoughts into the perverse directions I have described. Mr Mendel, in his way an erudite man, was undoubtedly capable of putting words in my mouth, but my mind was a private and a dirty place.

Poor Mr Mendel! He certainly earned his fee. If my interest was slight, my voice was non-existent. Every Monday and Wednesday evening, seated at the bow-legged table in his dining-room, we rehearsed my portion of the Torah.

"*V'zeh hadavar asher ta'aseh lohem l'kadesh,*" he sang like the star of *La Traviata.*

"*V'zeh hadavar asher . . .*" I repeated, a travesty.

Mr Mendel picked out each word with a silver pointer. This ended in a clenched fist, a single finger being outstretched. The direct relationship between digit and word emphasized the divine origin of the text, inspiration transformed into language without the intervention of a pen. Similarly, Mr Mendel was less concerned with the raiments of his body than with the condition of his soul, which was essentially that of a *shtetl* Jew. Nothing could shake his certainty, not even history. He had no interest in why something happened; he knew that the rise of National Socialism and the subsequent displacement of his person was due to neither economic nor sociological causes but to the wickedness of man. He never referred to the Germans, the English he still called "they". Yet Mr

Scriptophobia

Mendel read the *Daily Express* and lived in a Victorian terrace halfway down Greyhound Hill.

"Jacob, you are a Jewish boy," he said, "soon, please God, you will become a Jewish man. Then you must leave Hendon. Go, dwell among your people in Eretz Yisroel." Only now do I fully appreciate how lost Mr Mendel felt among the English-speaking goyim — even though the rabbi's house was just around the corner.

Taking advantage of this proximity, Rabbi Nathan frequently interrupted my lessons — not that I objected — in order to discuss the redecoration of the synagogue with Mr Mendel. I was supposed to practise by myself during these diversions but I found eavesdropping preferable, even though I didn't really grasp the significance of the debate.

"Where I come from," said Mr Mendel, "the *bima* was the heart of the shul, part of the pillar that supported the roof. Only in the West is it at the far end, almost a stage already. You are in danger of becoming remote, my friend, an orator or — God forbid — an actor."

"You are very astute, Mr Mendel," said Rabbi Nathan, "you have a nose for temptation."

"Too many rabbis have silver tongues," said Mr Mendel. "They give their words a shine, then sell them like the diamond merchants of Amsterdam. Take my advice, move the *bima* and speak from the heart."

Rabbi Nathan smiled. "Mr Mendel," he said, "I am almost persuaded."

The *bima*, I deduced, was the marble-fronted platform, the steps of which I would have to ascend in the not-too-distant future, provided that Mr Mendel succeeded, against all the odds, in preparing me sufficiently. Each Saturday morning I went through the motions in my mind, gradually instilling in myself the confidence of the hypnotized. But now Mr Mendel, of all people, seemed to want to take the ground from beneath my feet, and I felt a kind of vertigo as my previous certainty vanished.

I must have groaned or something, for I suddenly

25

attracted the attention of Rabbi Nathan.

"Just look at your pupil, Mr Mendel," he said, "he's as white as a sheet."

"What's the matter, Jacob?" asked Mr Mendel. "Here," he said, offering me his fancy box, "take a pinch of snuff. It'll clear your head."

Before I had a chance to respond there was a kerfuffle in the hallway, after which Mrs Mendel led in a second visitor. It was Helga.

"Oh, my God," said Mrs Mendel, "the boy has had a premonition. Here is his au pair with bad news."

Helga's cheeks were flushed from running the half-mile from our house. She must have left in a hurry because she was still wearing her apron. Although I was practically breathless with suspense I couldn't help remarking the sensational difference between Mrs Mendel and Helga. Helga radiated femininity, while Mrs Mendel hid whatever she had beneath a *sheitel*, a doleful countenance and a dumpy body. Rabbi Nathan was no less observant.

"For goodness' sake," he said, "tell us what has happened."

"The boy's dog," said Mrs Mendel, "it's been run over!"

I slumped forward, unconcerned about my sobbing, but desperate to conceal an absurdly prominent erection.

"Come," said Rabbi Nathan, "I'll drive you home."

My mother, slightly unhinged by the accident, thought that Rabbi Nathan had come to make the funeral arrangements. "The vet took the body away," she said. "We didn't want to upset Jacob any more than necessary. I never realized you would be involved. Are there special prayers for a dog?"

"Calm yourself, my dear," said the rabbi, "I am here unofficially. I was with Mr Mendel when your girl broke the news. I thought it best to bring your son home in my car."

"Oh," said my mother, "I am most grateful. Has Jacob thanked you?"

"Of course," he said.

Scriptophobia

"What happened?" I asked.

My mother began to cry. "Stupid dog! Stupid bloody dog! The postman knocked. So I opened the door. What else should I do? Before I knew what was happening he was in the road. Bang! That was that. He didn't suffer, thank God. Go on, say it's all my fault!"

Rabbi Nathan, having spotted the fatal package, addressed my mother. "You mustn't blame yourself, Mrs Silkstone," he said.

"I wasn't," she replied, "but he will."

"Perhaps it would be better to talk about something else," said the rabbi, "to take your minds off the tragedy. I believe you are looking forward to a happier event, your son's bar mitzvah." My mother nodded. "As you know," he continued, "it is customary for me to conclude my sermon on the blessed day with a homily directed at the boy and his family. I like to make them as personal as possible. What can you tell me about Joseph here?"

"*Jacob* is a good boy," said my mother, "he's very bright."

"Good," said the rabbi, "does he have any hobbies?"

"He likes to paint," replied my mother. "A couple of years ago he had a picture in the Children's Royal Academy. You must have seen his photograph in the *Hendon and Finchley Times*."

"Not that I recall," said Rabbi Nathan, "but I should like to see some of your son's work."

"Jacob," said my mother, "fetch your paintings to show the rabbi."

While I was sorting through the portfolios in my bedroom I heard a familiar order issued downstairs:

"Helga! Some tea for the rabbi. And don't forget that delicious Toblerone your mother sent from home."

Rabbi Nathan, it turned out, had a weakness for chocolate. He moistened his lips with the tip of his red tongue as Helga delicately separated the bar into its constituent triangles and dropped them on to an ornate plate where they looked like broken Stars of David. The

27

rabbi devoured piece after piece as he flicked through my watercolours, leaving chocolate fingerprints on those he liked best.

"These are excellent," he said. "God has granted you an exceptional talent. Use it, but never abuse it, and always give thanks where they are due." Then, as if struck by a sudden inspiration, he said: "We will soon be moving the *bima* to the centre of the synagogue. If I commission you to paint the shul now, before work begins, so we'll have a permanent record of how it looked, will you be able to do it?"

"Of course he will," said my mother.

Thus Rabbi Nathan became a regular visitor to our house, as he kept an eye on the progress of his picture, though sometimes I suspected he was more interested in Helga's confectionery. My parents were delighted but also terrified that he would discover her true nationality. But that was the least of Helga's secrets.

8

I still have the letter Rabbi Nathan wrote when the painting was eventually finished. Just looking at it makes me feel queasy, but here it is:

> Dear Jacob,
> Congratulations on your picture of the synagogue which your father brought to me the other day. I think it is a wonderful effort into which you must have put considerable time and concentration. I am having it framed and giving it a prominent position in my home. Continue the good work, Jacob.
> With kind regards, Rabbi Nathan.

Incidentally, the portrait was a very clumsy representation of reality, the neutral tones of the synagogue's interior being overwhelmed by my thick charcoal lines, but anyway it was decided to have a dinner in honour of its completion. Helga, being such a whiz in the kitchen, was asked to cook the meal.

"Perhaps you could do that wonderful veal dish," suggested my mother.

"With pleasure," said Helga.

"Mr Silkstone will give you as much money as you require," said my mother, "just let him know when you're off to the shops."

By chance I left school early that day and caught sight of Helga at the other end of Vivian Avenue. Rather than waving I decided to spy on her, fool that I was, so hid in a newsagent's till she went by. I followed like a lascivious lap-dog, past Leslie Mann and Martin's, the delicatessen, and across the road to where the older grocers traded.
Among them was the only non-kosher butcher left in Hendon Central.

Helga entered. I was invisible; would that I had vanished and been none the wiser. Instead I stood and watched the treacherous mime, obviously performed many times before, between Helga and the butcher's boy. She pointed, he reached, she nodded, he sliced, she sniffed, he wrapped, and she departed with four pounds of pork.

What to do? If I told my parents that they had been eating pork for over a year they would have grown tumours in their stomachs on the spot. Moreover, Helga would be kicked out for sure — impossible to contemplate in my state of erotomania. I wanted to leave well alone, but could I really connive in serving pork to a rabbi? What a decision!

That night, my parents being out, I carelessly neglected to lock the bathroom door as usual. When Helga stepped in I was stark naked, with an erection that reached my *pupik*. It was the straw that broke the camel's back.

"What do you want of me?" she demanded.

"Nothing," I replied.

"Always you are walking up and down in your knickers," she said. "Well, you are young. I ignore it. But now you go too far. I must speak with your parents."

"If you do," I said, "I'll tell them about the veal."

"What do you mean?" said Helga.

"I know it's really pork," I said.

"That's a lie," she said.

"I've seen you buy it," I replied.

Helga took a step toward me. "I'll do whatever you ask," she said.

Could I really say it? "Let me see your breasts."

Helga hesitated for a few moments, then raised her hands and pulled the red sweater over her head, allowing me to smell the deodorant that emanated from her smooth armpits. The static electricity that left wisps of her hair floating at right-angles to her all-but-bare shoulders communicated itself to my ecstatic body. I began to shiver.

Helga looked at me. "Shall I take off my brassière?" she asked.

I nodded, unnecessarily, for there wasn't one part of my person not in motion.

Helga fiddled behind her back with that garment of black lace, through which I could already make out the darker pink of her nipples, until the shoulder straps suddenly went slack and the material wrinkled like dead skin.

"Shut your eyes," said Helga.

When I looked again I could see her breasts gleaming in the neon light, as if they were brand new, and I felt as if I were seeing a woman in the third dimension for the first time. Not only did breasts have substance, they had variety, according to which way you looked at them.

"You are satisfied?" asked Helga, who would probably have removed her jeans as well, had I been bolder. "Oh, yes," she said, at last acknowledging my stiff little salute, "I can see that you are. It seems that my *kleine menshele* isn't so *kleine* after all. Do you want me to touch it?"

I didn't say no.

"Come," she said, "we must stand in the bath. We do not want to make a mess on your mother's fine new carpet."

Mess? Hitherto I had only experienced ecstasy in my sleep, and had a picture in my mind of an invisible spider, a denizen of darkness, emerging from the head in my

Scriptophobia

pyjama pants to spin a web out of the night's sticky dew, a thread of which was even now swaying gently between my legs. What else was there? The symptoms exhibited by my penis were beginning to frighten me, and I further tortured myself with the image of a banana stuffed with dynamite. Pity my poor parents as they come home only to find fragments of flesh clinging like bubblegum to the bathroom walls, the last remnants of their son's manhood, the last hope of the House of Silkstone. I wanted to cry, "Enough!" but it was too late, I was no longer my own master. I had no choice but to obey Helga, and so I stepped over the side into our pink bathtub, where Helga, a bar of soap in her wet hands, was already kneeling and knelt also at her command.

"I did not know that Jewish boys were so dirty," said Helga, as she coaxed the last secret from my body, thereby ensuring mutual silence.

Rabbi Nathan and his wife arrived at about eight the following evening. We usually dined in the breakfast-room, but tonight was hardly an orthodox occasion. In keeping with the importance of the event, my mother had polished up our best crockery, our silver cutlery and our Bohemian glasses; also she had pressed a fine cloth made of Venetian lace. All these she placed upon the Sun King-style table in the dining-room. Rabbi Nathan, shown every courtesy, was seated at the head, from where he recited the appropriate blessing over each dish as it appeared from the kitchen.

"This soup is exquisite," said the rabbi, addressing Helga, not God.

"Yes," said my mother, "it's a traditional Swiss recipe."

"As you know, the new bima was inaugurated last week," said the rabbi, mopping up his soup bowl with a chunk of pumpernickel, "and already I have forgotten what the old one looked like. It is indeed fortunate, Jacob, that I have your fine painting to remind me."

"It looks beautiful in our lounge," added his wife, "everyone admires it."

31

I blushed. Misinterpreting my embarrassment, they all chuckled. The real cause was the appearance of Helga bearing the main course.

"Don't worry," joked my father, "the cream isn't real."

She placed the steaming platter in front of the rabbi, who said a blessing which must have fallen upon deaf ears. As he lifted the first forkful to his mouth I felt helpless, as if in a nightmare, forced to witness — but unable to prevent — a loved one going to their doom.

"What's the matter with you, Jacob?" said my mother, between mouthfuls. "Why aren't you eating your veal?"

To whom should I confess? Mr Mendel? As if to atone for my transgression, I became a compliant pupil, much to his astonishment.

"Mrs Mendel," he said, when his wife brought him tea and cookies, "it looks like Jacob has decided to become a *mensh* after all. Caruso he'll never be, but he'll do on the day."

My performance in the synagogue, however, was only the first part of the ordeal; next would come the party at the Café Royal.

One day my father, no stranger to the East End, took me down to his crony in Brick Lane who was printing the invitations. The shop hadn't been redecorated since it opened in the reign of Queen Victoria. The owner, standing over the presses in the back room, caught sight of my father and rushed out to greet him.

"Dave, Dave," he said, "you are such a stranger. What a pity the old lady is away today, it'll break her heart that she missed you." He wiped his inky fingers on his filthy apron and pinched my cheek. "So this is the famous young man, at last," he said. "Tell me, Jacob, are you bringing your parents *naches*?"

"What's *naches*?" I asked.

"*Gevalt!*" he cried. "The boy doesn't know Yiddish."

My father smiled. "It's enough trouble to teach him Hebrew," he said. "Anyway, Yiddish belongs to the old country."

"Pooh," said the printer, "he lives in Hendon a few years and already Yiddish isn't good enough for him." He looked at me. "Well, boychick, what do you want to be when you grow up? An accountant?"

"No," I replied, "a writer."

"*Mazeltov*," he cried, "if I am still alive, please God, I'll be your printer. We'll show up those no-good Hendon-niks for what they are — imitation Jews."

"That's enough," said my father. "He used to be a Communist," he added, by way of explanation.

As we drove back along Whitechapel High Street my father said: "If you're such a big shot with a pen, how come I've got to write your speech for you?"

9

He had a point. When I stood up at the Top Table of the Louis Suite in the Café Royal on 21 May 1961 to respond to my uncle's toast, the words I uttered were not my own. What did I have to say to my relatives, all of whom now sat facing me in their finery?

"My dear parents, Grandmother, Reverend Sir, relatives and friends," I began, "one expects my uncle to conjure up words and phrases as he is a member of the Magic Circle, but it is more difficult for me to reply. However, I should like to take the opportunity of thanking you all most sincerely for coming along today and contributing towards making this such a memorable occasion. To my mum and dad I would like to express my heartfelt thanks for providing me with everything a boy can desire, most of all a love and understanding that has always been such a help to me, especially in my younger days. To my dear mum, please forgive me if I do not always finish my meals, but tonight I certainly shall. To my dad, who is such a friend to me, I will do my best to fulfil all your hopes. My grateful thanks, also, to my nanny and to all my uncles and aunts who make up my wonderful family. I cannot conclude without expressing my thanks to my Hebrew teacher, Mr Mendel, whose patience was rewarded yesterday, and to Rabbi Nathan, whose profound remarks will always be an inspiration to me. Thank you all."

There were cries of "Hear! Hear!" as I fell back into my padded chair. I smiled at Helga, sitting at a distant table among my teenage cousins, and silently thanked her as well — for showing me her tits.

Actually they weren't exactly under wraps at the moment. Sexy Helga was as desirable as a convertible VW to all the younger Silkstones, who competed for her favours while the Rudy Rome Orchestra performed a Chubby Checker medley. Their elders, on the other hand, shuddered with disapproval at her décolletage. I dutifully danced with my mother, both of us in specially tailored outfits, she having revived the sequin industry for the occasion. My own suit had taken the best cutter in Edgware weeks to sew, but still looked ungainly on me.

"Are you enjoying yourself?" asked my mother.

"You're joking," I replied.

Meanwhile Helga had graduated to demonstrating the tango with one of my bolder uncles. As I watched, it occurred to me that her undulations were secretly transmitting the meaning of life; that everything was a delusion or a drudge except the animal pleasure of copulation. Without realizing it, my parents had invited a Lorelei to my bar mitzvah. What else could she do but wreck it? My most disreputable relative — a receiver of stolen goods — having indulged beyond his capacity, waltzed over to where she was sitting and planted a tulip in her cleavage and a kiss upon her cheek.

Rabbi Nathan, as always, was more ambitious. Who knows? Perhaps he had been planning the assault all evening. Certainly he was too preoccupied to notice the flamboyant black eye, the subject already of heroic legend, which had definitely not been there when he had last seen me, at the kiddush after yesterday's bar-mitzvah service. My parents, who could hardly tell him the truth, but

34

couldn't bring themselves to say that I had slipped on a bar
of soap in the bathroom either, breathed a sigh of relief —
somewhat prematurely.

10

As a matter of fact Rabbi Nathan had been uncharacteristi-
cally absentminded at the kiddush itself, so much so that
he lost count of the sherries he drank, and almost forgot to
leave. Perhaps he found our armchairs too comfortable or
our honey cake too tempting; either way, there he sat,
dozing in state beneath the mantelpiece, deaf to the hints
of our chiming clock, which informed me, hands out-
spread in despair, that Wingate's last match of the season
was going to kick off in fifteen minutes. My father was as
desperate as me, not wanting to miss his biggest game
since the great victory of 1940, but what could we do
except curse fate for fixing the second leg of the London
League Cup Final on the same day as my bar mitzvah?

"It's God's punishment for all those other Saturdays
when you rushed to football behind the rabbi's back," said
my mother when she found us plotting in the kitchen, her
superstition getting the better of her sympathy.

"You make me sick!" I cried. "Jews make me sick!'

"In that case," said my father, "tell me why you are in
such a hurry to get to Wingate?"

Had I then known Heine's famous poem, "Prinzess in
Sabbat", describing the canine curse upon a Prince named
Israel which goes —

> Dog with the thoughts of a dog, all week he slinks
> cowering through the garbage and filth of life, mocked
> at by street urchins.

> Yet every Friday evening, in the hour of twilight,
> suddenly the spell is loosed, and the dog becomes
> once more a human creature.

Man, with human feelings, with uplifted head and heart, festively, almost cleanly dressed, he walks into his father's hall.

— I might have understood the question a little better. Although he went to synagogue for my sake, my father no longer possessed any real religious beliefs. Yet he thought of himself as Jewish, and was only fully alive when he could express those sentiments. So for "Friday evening" read "Saturday afternoon", and for "father's hall" read "Wingate Football Club". Soccer may seem a poor substitute for religion, but it alone provided that missing sense of community. Religion, race or culture? It wasn't a question that bothered the anti-Semites who saved us that afternoon. For suddenly there was Mr Mendel knocking at our front door breathless with the news that vandals had daubed swastikas on the synagogue walls. Even then I do not think Rabbi Nathan would have left if Mr Mendel hadn't insisted.

"Rabbi," he said, "the police are waiting."

"Forgive me, Jacob," said Rabbi Nathan as I showed him to the door.

I would have forgiven Hitler at that moment.

As soon as the rabbi's coat-tails were out of sight we ran along the Watford Way and reached Hall Lane just as the referee was blowing his whistle (a silver one, donated by our rivals, whispered his detractors) to signal the start of the game. Our opponents were a team from London's docklands, whose reputation as the dirtiest in amateur football was well earned. Their supporters expected nothing less. Rumour had it that among their number was the organizer of a dog-doping racket, a hit-man responsible for several underworld murders, and Bruno Gascoyne's bodyguard — the rest being merely pickpockets, prostitutes and other choice members of the lumpier proletariat. The first leg, at their ground, had been a goalless draw, much to the surprise of everyone, not least the referee. In fact we had the ball in the net a couple of times, but each was disallowed for the suspiciously spurious reason that one or other of our forwards had been offside, a manifest injustice since their left-back had been caught napping on the goal-line in both instances.

"What's the matter, ref?" we shouted. "Forgot your specs?"

But our outrage knew no bounds when he awarded a penalty against us, still an unusual circumstance, with less than five minutes to go.

"What was that for?" we cried, echoing Job and his equally maltreated descendants, but the black-shirted little dictator didn't have to justify himself to the likes of us. Ignoring our pleas and those of our representatives, the players, he placed the ball on the white spot, into whose circumference the whole earth was suddenly sucked.

We held our breath, conscious that we were witnessing one of those pivotal moments in history when worlds are won or lost. In November 1932 Germany could have either gone to the left or the right. We prayed that our goalkeeper would make a wiser decision. He did, good socialist that he was.

"You won't be so lucky next time," chanted our opponents, and we believed them.

"*Mazeltov*," said all my father's cronies as we took our usual places on the touchline, though it was uncertain whether they were congratulating us upon our perfectly timed arrival or my bar mitzvah. Either way we had little to cheer about on the field, as our defence inexplicably succumbed to collective self-doubt and conceded two goals in as many minutes.

"That's the Father and the Son," taunted our opponents, "now let's complete the Trinity."

Their centre-forward obliged at that killing moment just before half-time. Ironically he picked up the ball on the rebound from our best attack of the afternoon. Our outside-right (known as the Jewish Stanley Matthews) suddenly came to life and set off on one of his vertiginous runs, pausing *en route* to offer the ball to their defenders, only to leave them lunging at empty air, before sending over a perfect cross that our centre-forward hit mid-stride. Their goalkeeper had no idea what was going on, but it didn't matter, because the ball hit his body, bounced back into play and ended up in our goal instead.

There was just enough time for a last attack before the half ended and again we nearly scored. Once more our right-winger made his markers look like monkeys, much to the delight of our opponents, who could now afford to cheer this quicksilver Jewboy and mock their own golem-like backs; but the move led to nothing. We hid from them at half-time, fearing their condescension more than their antagonism. We chanted, "WIN-GATE! WIN-GATE!" with all our might when the teams reappeared, to cheer ourselves up as much as the players.

"What do you think the manager said to them in the changing-room?" I asked my father.

" 'The Lord is with thee, thou mighty men of valour,' " he replied, repeating the words Wingate had said to him all those years ago.

If so they worked a treat. Straight from the kick-off our hyped-up outside right, in real life a tailor, ran down the wing like a sewing-machine through satin. "Shoot! Shoot!" we screamed as his pass floated over the heads of the defenders and landed precisely on the toecap of our centre-forward, who tapped the ball into the air and kicked it as if it were the head of Eichmann. "GOAL!" we screamed, then: "WIN-GATE! WIN-GATE!" as the game restarted.

Now I don't want to sound like a mystic, but I swear I sensed that our concentrated will-power was beginning to turn the game around, though it was only after we scored our second goal that I dared believe it.

They had laughed at our overweight inside-left before the interval, called him Fatman and worse, but now the joke was on them, as he demonstrated the superiority of the mind over the foot. Trapping a loose ball, he strolled in the general direction of the opposing goal, brushing off the frequent challenges as if by accident, and then in the blink of an eye split their defence wide open with a clinical pass. Whereupon our centre-forward, obviously a mind-reader, appeared as if out of nowhere and booted the ball past their bewildered goalkeeper.

There followed a crazed period when we drove our team on and they responded with attack after attack from every position, but the third goal would not come, despite a dozen near-misses. And then, just as we began to doubt the outcome, our team's momentum began to die, and the narrow escapes began to occur around our goal. Men about me began to shake their heads sadly. Some, unable to bear the suspense, kept looking at their watches as if trying to see into the future.

"Only ten minutes to go," said my father. "If they score again we'll be finished."

Determined to contradict that gloomy prophecy, we began to chant with renewed vigour loudly enough to waken the dead, let alone a deflated football team. Whatever the reason our outside-right swiftly intercepted a bad pass, sewed the ball to his boot with a couple of flicks, and began to sprint toward their goal; jumping over lunging feet, dodging illegal tackles, onward ran the hero, until there was no one left between him and the goalkeeper. Last week the linesman's flag would have gone up for sure, but not today.

"What's different?" I wondered.

"Only that we invited Sir Stanley Rous, president of FIFA, himself a former referee, to present the Cup. Smart move, eh?" said the Prince of Shmattes.

For a moment it looked as if his presence would be unnecessary, as our winger tripped, staggered forward and seemed to lose the ball, at which the goalkeeper relaxed slightly and moved to collect it. A big mistake, for our man suddenly accelerated, leaped over the goalie's diving hands and drove the ball into the empty net. Oh, Lord! The equalizer. We went wild with delight. But the relief broke our concentration and made our players careless, allowing the unthinkable to happen.

An unnecessary back pass found one of their forwards instead of our goalkeeper. We watched, horrified, as the ball flew past him. How their supporters gloated! Considering all the circumstances carefully, we embraced nihilism and concluded that the universe was an absurd dump devoid of meaning. What was the point of our sensational fight-back if we were destined to be defeated? And so the match ran down, and time ran out, as did our fair-weather supporters, though they soon turned back at the gate when they heard our enormous cheer.

Standing some thirty yards from goal, our inside-left had casually hit a ball with such force that the net broke upon receipt. We were level again. Only a couple of minutes remained. The next goal would be the decider. "Dear God," I prayed, "if you let us score the winning goal I swear to have nothing more to do with Helga. Someone else can have her!"

It must have been coincidence, but immediately thereafter our goalkeeper, having just made a sensational save, threw the ball to our left-back who passed it to our right-back who passed it to our left-half and so on, until it arrived at the feet of our centre-forward, *without anyone having moved on either side.* The ball left as quickly as it had come, and no one in the ground had any doubts as to its destination, so clearly was "goal" written all over it. A few seconds later and the referee blew the final whistle. Wingate had taken the London League Cup in miraculous fashion!

"It's a pity Hitler didn't finish the lot of 'em off," said a peroxide blonde in a fake leopard-skin coat and toreador pants, unable to stomach the sight of Jews rejoicing.

"Fucking bitch," I replied. At which she dispensed with language and slapped me around the face. So I slapped her back — placing my father in an untenable position; I had used foul language and struck a woman, indefensible acts, but the provocation was undeniable.

"Jacob," he said, "do not sink to the level of this scum."

Scriptophobia

I wanted to inform him that scum rises, but was only able to demonstrate that Jews tend to fall down when hit in the eye by bums with fists the size of hams.

"Just who are you calling scum, you old cocksucker?" said the Christian gentleman as he approached my father. "My wife happens to be the Cha-Cha Queen of Tilbury and you are going down on your knees pronto to beg her forgiveness."

Listen, I was never so stupid as to expect my father to whip a monster like that single-handed. As I have said, boxing was not my father's forte, and I would not have blamed him if he had gone down and kissed that whore's pumps, which he might well have done if Al Pinsky hadn't stepped in. Now Al wasn't very big, which amused the bully, who was so cocksure that I decided to withhold the fact that Al Pinsky was once the lightweight champion of Great Britain. His friends probably told him when he woke up in hospital, so he wouldn't feel quite so bad about being knocked cold by a Jew.

Later that night Helga offered me two pieces of flesh: raw steak for my eye, which I accepted; her body for my manhood, which I refused. I didn't dare break my promise to God so soon. I left that sort of thing to Rabbi Nathan.

11

Towards the end of my bar-mitzvah party, when the Rudy Rome Orchestra was already playing lachrymose melodies, Helga suddenly broke away from her over-romantic partner and ran towards the Ladies' Powder Room. Heady with wine and the whirl of the dance, I gave chase, hoping to end the evening with a passionate embrace, and so burst into the enchanted chamber with its pink sinks, neon lights, and mirrors that multiplied my desire a thousand times.

My clones searched in every corner but it soon became clear that we were the only inhabitants, until I heard a grunt arise from the inner sanctum where the cubicles were situated. Surely Helga's bowel movements were not that strenuous? Indeed they weren't, for investigation quickly revealed the source as unmistakably male. But which of my relatives would have the nerve to lock Helga in one of the lavatories in order to manhandle her private parts?

I entered the adjoining cubicle and stood upon the mahogany seat so that I could see over the partition. Helga was there sitting on the toilet with her breasts exposed. More unexpected was the sight of Rabbi Nathan, trousers around his ankles, trying to force his defrocked member into her mouth. It was not pleasure I experienced in seeing hypocrisy thus unmasked but shock, so great a shock that I cried out loud. Rabbi Nathan jumped, as though the admonition had come from Heaven itself, and those parts of his body which had been relaxed became as if petrified and those parts which had been stiff became limp.

Helga, still open-mouthed despite the sudden detumescence, recovered her composure the quickest and calmly repositioned her dress with her thumbs, unbolted the door, and was gone, leaving the rabbi and his disciple to explain themselves as best they could. Meanwhile Helga, somewhat dishevelled, re-entered the ballroom and, dislodging my father, flung herself sobbing into my mother's arms. She was quickly escorted to a discreet corner, where she privately revealed the cause of her extraordinary behaviour.

"It's a slander," said my mother, "this girl is nothing but a harlot and an anti-Semite. May God forgive me for employing a German!"

"Are you sure it was Rabbi Nathan?" asked my father.

Helga nodded.

"Liar," hissed my mother.

There was, it must be said, a certain poetic justice in the attempted fellatio, a fitting punishment for Helga's own dietary transgressions; even so, I couldn't let Rabbi Nathan get away with it, for Helga, with nothing to lose, might betray me.

"She's telling the truth," I said, "I saw what happened."
Then there was nothing for it but to fetch Rabbi Nathan.

"My life is in your hands," he said.

No one slept in the Silkstone household that night.

"Perhaps he was trying to take revenge upon Germany through its daughters," was the best excuse my father could find.

"He thought she was Swiss," I replied.

Finally my mother broke the stalemate. "Helga," she said, "what do you want us to do?"

"Whatever you think best," she replied. "I am not a vindictive person. And, though it sounds strange, I am grateful to Rabbi Nathan. Because of his behaviour I no longer feel guilty for what my people did to the Jews."

"In that case we will hush it up," said my mother. "Not another word about Rabbi Nathan's folly. You understand? Not a word!"

12

History is full of defensive stratagems that failed. Wingate wasn't fooled for a minute by the Maginot Line — "The Germans can cross it at will," he said — nor did the Bar Lev line stop the Egyptians when they chose to attack in 1973, the same year that I finally decided to ignore my mother's injunction and write *Rabbi Nathan's Folly*. My parents were not amused.

"Are you satisfied?" asked my mother, pointing to an empty bottle of Valium, beside which was cast the offending manuscript, like a suicide note. "Why don't you write something nice about the Jews," she said, "instead of *dreck* like this?"

"There are plenty of others to do that," I said. "Besides, you are confusing fact with fiction. I write stories."

"So tell a story," said my father, "and don't make a laughing-stock of Rabbi Nathan."

"Our son is well-named," said my mother, "his words

are like silk, but his heart is a stone. He'll publish it, if he
can. May his arm drop off!''

Writing is one thing, publishing another. In the end I
took *Rabbi Nathan's Folly* to the printer in Whitechapel
and reminded him of his promise. He hadn't forgotten.

And so it came to pass that my first novel was launched
in a prefabricated scout hut hired by the local Communist
Party under the guise of the Society for the Perpetuation of
Radical Literature. This didn't con the British Party, who
sent a few hecklers along to wave Union Jacks and spit at
the guests. Unfortunately they wasted their time; no one
came, only the faithful, numbering less than a score.

Such factual niceties didn't bother the proprietor of the
newly formed Potemkin Press, who held his first title aloft
and announced:

"This book will shake the Anglo-Jewish establishment
to its foundations, a richly deserved fate. For writing this
courageous novel my friend Jake will take a lot of shtick
from vested interests, but I tell you that ordinary Jews from
Whitechapel to Hendon should go on their knees and give
him thanks. The so-called Oil Crisis is the beginning of the
end, the final crisis of capitalism as prophesied by Karl
Marx. The tragedy is that the Jews, once the backbone of
the socialist movement, have become identified with the
Gentile Establishment in the eyes of the working people.
When the revolution comes, as it must, and the bloodsuckers have fled to their tax-free havens, it is their Jewish
poodles who will be torn limb from limb. I remember being
at a meeting when the chairman — a prominent Jewish
banker — pointed to a member of the audience and said,
'Mr X, the whole community is proud of your elevation to
the Cabinet.' In a Tory administration! 'No,' I cried, 'I'm
ashamed. A good Jew should turn down such honours.' I
was booed, naturally. But I was right. Listen to them
outside, baying for our blood. Now they are weak and we
are safe — *we*, the fighters, will always be safe, but who
will defend the other Jews when their protectors have
slunk off like thieves in the night? They are doomed, I tell

you, unless, unless . . . we can find more brave souls like Jake here willing to smash the golden calf of materialism. Their leaders are hypocrites, and in their vanity and their folly they are dragging their people to disaster. Until we stop them with this" — he pointed to my book — "our most powerful weapon!"

His eloquence persuaded ten souls to purchase copies there and then, so far as I know the only volumes that were ever sold. I was glad to note that among the buyers was Lena, my publisher's only daughter, and I was even happier when she asked me to sign it. But then a peculiar thing happened to the people's hero: he lost control of his right hand, so that the pen took off across the title-page like a cardiograph. I had never acquired, during adolescence, the habit of drinking coffee; my hand shook so much it was impossible to get a cup near my lips. But it had never stopped me writing before. Now I couldn't even print my name.

"Are you feeling OK?" asked Lena.

"I think so," I replied.

"You don't look it," she said.

I tried again, but a trained chimpanzee could have done it better.

Sweat dripped down my wrists, my hands shook worse than ever, my heart palpitated, the room revolved. A mother's curse is no joke. So let us give it a technical name: scriptophobia. Thereafter it was only with the utmost difficulty that I was able to put my ideas down on paper, concentrating on the form to such an extent that the content got lost. Why didn't I use a typewriter, you're probably thinking. I'll tell you, it was even worse. The letters danced on the page, copulating indiscriminately in strange combinations. I had, in short, lost my voice, for only when my thoughts were written down did they fully exist. Let's be more succinct. I had been gagged, or maybe I had chastened myself in anticipation of the worse punishment that awaited me. *Rabbi Nathan's Folly* turned out to be my folly too.

My subsequent attempts at self-expression were more modest. Incognito, wearing nothing but a raincoat and sandals, I entered Sunnyhill Park, having visited my parents in more conventional attire, and scandalized a new generation of Philippina-eyed housegirls with a sight of the real me. Why not? Wingate, I am told, frequently welcomed visitors in his natural state.

II Dermagraphia

1

Have I mentioned my hives? Thanks to them I looked like a map of the world in the days of the British Empire on the night I first fucked Lena. It was seven years since our first meeting, and three weeks after our reunion. In the intervening period I worked as a copywriter in a large advertising agency, an ideal venue for a man with vision but no voice of his own.

Or I did until the Creative Director called me into his office and fired me.

"Why?" I demanded.

"We've fallen on hard times," he said, "someone's got to go."

"Why me?" I asked.

"Do you really want to know?" he said.

"Yes," I said.

"Right," he said. "It's because I don't like your face. Seeing it makes me feel miserable. You look as if you don't know the meaning of the word fun. I've watched you with clients. No wonder we're losing business. Instead of oozing with enthusiasm you act as though you'd just stepped into a pile of dog shit. And that's not all. The rest of you looks like a skeleton on stilts. Don't you eat or something? You asked, 'Why me?' My answer is, 'Who else?' Goodbye, Jake."

The bastard was right. What did I know about joy?

Since the publication of my book — though psychoanalysts may insist upon looking elsewhere for the "remote origins" — I had been the locus of a civil war between mind and body. Whose side was I on? The body's, I suppose. After all, my life would have been a lot easier if I didn't always have to cope with psychosomatic assaults on the pleasure principle. But why did my mind have it in for my body? Was it paying it back for those early victories, when it allied itself with Germany, or was it a spy implanted by my parents before birth, to be activated at the first signs of independence?

It was generally possible to link each affliction with a particular event, as in the case of my scriptophobia. So what caused my hives? Easy. The prospect of sex. And the more I wanted it, the redder I became. Lena should have been very flattered.

We became reacquainted at the Institute of Contemporary Arts, where the notorious American novelist Jerry Unger was discussing his latest book with someone called Clive Sinclair. I still have the ticket, dated 19 February 1980. I took a seat beside the most attractive woman in the room. To my surprise she spoke.

"You should be up there," she whispered, "you're the English Unger."

"Where's the evidence?" I asked. She removed a copy of *Rabbi Nathan's Folly* from her bag and showed me the flyleaf with its contorted scrawl — the last words of Jake Silkstone that was.

"Lena!" I cried.

"The same," she said. "I was going to recommend your book to Unger. Now I'll be able to introduce the author as well."

Fortunately Sinclair asked Unger so many questions there was no time for anyone else to get a look in. Afterwards Lena tried to attract Unger's attention; he winked but didn't stop.

She did better with me. Three weeks later we were in bed together.

If you're wondering how a man in my condition managed to seduce such a beauty, the answer is: I didn't. She seduced me. As I sank into her belly I thought, *At last I have found peace.* My body wanted her and my mind let me have her.

Our wedding was nothing like my bar mitzvah. Her father didn't print the invitations. Mine didn't write the speeches. The tailors of Edgware knew us not, neither did the dressmakers of Finchley. We married in a register

Dermagraphia

office and bought a house in St Albans. Lena found work at the local comprehensive school. I sat at home writing samizdat literature. Amazing! I had achieved the impossible, a normal life.

Then one day Lena came home and said, "You'll have to get a job, I'm pregnant."

"Fine," I said, "what do you suggest?"

That was Lena's second surprise. "One of my old boyfriends is the editor of the *Jewish Voice*," she said, "I still see him from time to time. He tells me that his literary editor is retiring. He's willing to appoint you."

"Why?" I enquired.

"Because I asked him," she replied.

2

So here I am, the literary editor of the *Jewish Voice*, spokesman for the very values I was meant to have destroyed. It is, I suppose, a sort of poetic justice, to have ended up as a ventriloquist's dummy. At least I get invited to a lot of parties, the latest being a summons from Uzi, Cultural Attaché at the Israel Embassy in Palace Green, to a reception in honour of Ziz, the famous Polish poet.

Hold on! A Polish poet being fêted in Israel's Embassy? Is this a fantasy? On the contrary, it is *realpolitik*. Enticingly disguised, of course, by the glittering company — itself homogenized by black tie and evening gown — that has been assembled in the elegant Georgian room. The ornaments, collected from the Middle East, mysteriously complement the mansion's origins; they also have been painlessly assimilated. Yemenite silver rests upon an Adam mantelpiece, Turkish copper bowls set off a Grinling Gibbons fireplace. Persian rugs merge into the stone pavements beneath our feet, while crocodile-teared chandeliers shower light upon us. The latter lull us into admiring the clarity of our vision, whereas in truth we can't even see what's going on under our noses. For example, how many of tonight's revellers know the real reason for this extravaganza?

49

Certainly not the dark-skinned beauties in diaphanous veils who recline upon ottomans and *chaises-longues* like concubines in a seraglio, under the influence — it should be said — not of Israeli wine but of the cruder spirit of Polish vodka. Nor the intellectual gigolos whose necks strain giraffe-like better to spot the famous face or the easy lay. Though my wife leads a life of monogamous obscurity these scouts bypass the Levantine distractions to stand in her penumbra, where they are magically transformed into laughing hyenas. Who can blame them?

Around her throat my wife wears a silver chain from which two bluebirds hang. There is very little else between them and her breasts. These are especially prominent at present, for she is still giving milk to our son, although he is eighteen months old. Her low-cut dress, which consequently begins several inches from her body, is held upright by two shoulder-straps; both of which seem anxious to demonstrate the attraction of gravity. Uzi, the personification of levity, determines to give them a helping hand.

Creeping toward my wife — through the shifting maze that begins with Their Excellencies the Ambassadors Ben Zion and Polski, erstwhile compatriots, and includes a variety of dignitaries, apes of the Anglo-Saxon establishment, and their wives, for whom, in distant lands, black men unearthed diamonds and gold and mulberry-eating worms wove silk, and ends at Ziz in his turtle-necked sweater who stands, as it happens, within arm's length of the straps — he reaches out, his hooked fingers acting as levators, and down goes her dress.

At first I think Lena has fainted, until I see that I have two wives. The most prominent stands gleaming and pink in the limelight of a hundred eyes, her arms crossed over her chest, leaving her flawless skin unprotected save for a pair of transparent briefs. A glass of white wine, still in her hand, now rests at an acute angle, so that the contents trickle out. Uzi kneels, mouth agape, to catch the drops, like a tourist at a Dionysian shrine, until I break the spell and cover my wife. Lena, formerly a teacher, more used to staff dinners than these bohemian junkets, insists upon leaving, despite Uzi's profuse apologies.

"All right," he says. "But you have not yet met Ziz. That I insist upon."

"My dear," cries Ziz, pressing her hand to his lips, "never have I seen such a spectacular demonstration of the soul separated from the body. It has confirmed what I have always maintained. Our souls are not useless ectoplasm. No! They resemble the most desirable figures our minds can conjure up. Sweet lady, make me immortal with a kiss."

My wife, somewhat mollified, obliges.

"Let me tell you, dear lady," whispers Ziz in mock confidentiality, "for you I would defect tomorrow. It is correct that I have a family in Poland. But true passion — for God, for poetry, for a woman — is worth nothing unless you are prepared to sacrifice your first-born for it." He turns to me. "Don't you agree?"

"You have hit upon the difference between poetry and prose," I reply. "I write prose, therefore I must consider what my words mean before I utter them."

"Young man," says Ziz, "in my country that distinction is not recognized."

I do not answer. For I know that Ziz speaks from experience.

3

Just after the Second World War he published a series of sonnets, standard in form but extraordinary in substance. Instead of addressing the Motherland as a suitor might, the convention of the time, Ziz spoke to the Jews. His message was simple: "Come home." The regime's lackeys accused him of conspiring with cosmopolitan elements in an effort to blacken Poland's name, and thereby disguise the real culprit: Germany. But, miraculously, Ziz survived. There were rumours that he had protection in the highest circles;

Stalin himself was said to be frightened of touching him. To the effect that Ziz became known in the West as the Kremlin's court jester, its tame liberal.

However, in 1967 he ran into more trouble. "Suddenly," wrote Ziz in one of his famous essays for *Encounter*, "anti-Semitism was no longer voluntary, as it had been in the good old days, now it was compulsory. Even though there were no more Jews! In short, as you say, the Polish economy had gone down the tubes and the government needed a scapegoat. General Mieczyslaw Moczar, the Minister of Internal Affairs, orchestrated a witch-hunt of all the un-Polish Poles who had, in his eyes, master-minded Poland's collapse. At the same time, Tadeusz Walichnowski, head of the Nationalities Department in Moczar's ministry, published a book which revived the old slander of German-Jewish connivance in dumping the guilt for the Final Solution upon Poland."

Ziz spoke up — let us add — for such Jews as wished to remain in Poland and, inevitably, he fell foul of his old enemies. They got their chance on the evening of 6 June 1967, which Ziz spent in the company of a few theatrical cronies at SPATIF, a club for actors and suchlike in his home city of Cracow. All got blind drunk, naturally, despite the bloodthirsty images flickering across the television screen in the bar. The following week Vladyslav Machejek, a local hack, printed a piece in his anti-Semitic rag, during the course of which Ziz was accused of having toasted Israel's victory. Poland's ties with Israel were put on ice, likewise Ziz got the cold shoulder. For the best part of a decade he was out of print.

Now, however, there are rumours that Poland is keen to resume relations with Israel as soon as the situation permits. Hence this party. Ziz, also back in circulation, is an unofficial emissary, a sort of go-between. At any rate he has certainly eased relations between my wife, child of Lubliners, and Uzi, a Sabra.

4

Uzi, who has the looks of Peter Lorre and the energy of a chimpanzee, prances alongside my wife *en route* to the chopped liver *en croute*.

Ziz, remaining beside me, shakes his head. "The Jews," he says. "What a loss; we could do with a few like him in Poland now. It has become such a dull place. I blame it all on the Pope."

"Aren't you Catholic?" I ask.

"So?" he says. "Would you like the Chief Rabbi breathing down your neck all the time?"

We make ourselves comfortable, a newly opened bottle of Slivovitz of Szatmar between us, and talk as if the world were merely an observatory in which writers were granted total immunity.

"When I first walked into Marks & Spencer," says Ziz, "I nearly had an orgasm on the spot. So much lingerie, so many bras and panties! Invisible girls began to perform lascivious pantomimes before my eyes! In Cracow all you will see in such a department is one black brassière of gigantic proportions, rising like the Tatras from drapes of orange velvet. Hardly the stuff of oleaginous dreams. My friend, you have a beautiful wife. Forgive me, but I could not help noticing her charms. Tell me, how do you keep her?"

"What do you mean?" I ask.

"Please," says Ziz, "I did not mean to offend. You said before you are a writer. Always I have heard that in England writers do not earn very much. I meant, how do you make a living?"

"Easy," I say. "I am the literary editor of the *Jewish Voice*."

"In that case," says Ziz, "I have a present for you."

So saying, he removes a pad from his jacket pocket and, borrowing my fountain pen, begins to write. The lines, being short, suggest a poem.

"For your paper," says Ziz. "A token of good will

between Pole and Jew. You may print it free of charge. Please inform your wife that I have privately dedicated it to her. With your permission, of course. It is in Polish, I am afraid. But I am sure there are many in your building who speak both Polish and English."

5

Well, there's Asa Dorfman, formerly a taxi-driver, now the doorman, imprisoned for attempted murder. Born in Lodz in 1909, Asa, a hot-blooded child, had been a member of Betar, the youth wing of militant Zionism. One day he was sunbathing beside a river upon which women from the local Maccabe rowing club were showing off their skills. Asa watched for a time until, made drowsy by the beer and heat, he dozed off among the bumblebees and cornstalks. He awoke to what he thought was a Bacchanalia; for he observed, in the distance, centaurs in pursuit of flimsily clad females. But when he arose to ascertain the reality of the vision he saw, by the river bank, other black-shirted youths smashing the women's upturned sculls. Having learned the value of blood and iron as a panacea for insecurity, Asa removed an illegal revolver from his satchel and strode toward the xenophobic Endeks. A few shots quickly dispersed the thugs, who promptly reported the Jewish vigilante to the militia. This heroic deed, for which he served time, established a permanent model for Asa's political behaviour which, in turn, now determines the way he treats visitors to the *Jewish Voice*. Hence his honorary position as Chief of Security.

Asa, a naturalized Briton, naturally votes Tory. Not so Old Maxie, the office postman. Old Maxie, born in Smolensk years before the Revolution, is an unapologetic Stalinist, whose last ambition is to give Asa apoplexy, in which he will probably succeed.

Then there's Meir the Printer, whose only remaining function is to fix the Xerox machine when it gets jammed. In his spare time he edits, single-handed, an émigré

Dermagraphia

magazine which he makes up on his antique Yiddish typewriter and runs off on the office copier after hours. Everyone knows about it, but how do you accuse a man who survived Auschwitz of stealing ink and paper?

When I enter the building, the poem in my wallet, they are gathered around Asa Dorfman's desk, discussing the show trial of a Jewish writer, recently sentenced in Warsaw. According to Asa he is a martyr, a genius, incarcerated because he dared proclaim his Jewishness.

"You are talking through your hat," says Old Maxie. "He broke the law, that's why he's inside. Dialectical materialism is no different from the market forces you swear by. Everyone gets what they deserve. In his case it was five years."

"Maybe he did, maybe he didn't," says Meir the Printer, "I'm not saying. But I'll tell you this: he's no writer. After his arrest he polished off a few satirical sketches. Some found their way to my magazine. They are of very poor quality, believe me. But, thanks to them, he now has the status of persecuted writer. It's no use getting angry, Mr Doorman. Even in Poland there may be Jewish crooks. I have read the transcript of the trial — it is rare for the authorities to make public such a thing — and I believe he did what they say."

"Fool!" cries Asa. "Dupe of the anti-Semites!"

These are the potential translators of Ziz. To choose between such congenital dissenters without causing offence would have taxed the judgement of Paris and the wisdom of Solomon. I have neither. Secretly I ask Meir the Printer to do the job. Meanwhile, in my office, I write up the conversation with Ziz, which I had been unable to complete at home.

6

My wife, a forgiving sort, had spent the remainder of the party with Uzi, while Ziz and I got drunker and drunker until, finally, we swore undying friendship. When we returned home my wife, stimulated by the attention she had received and, despite herself, aroused by the fact that a roomful of strangers had seen her nakedness, wanted to make love. She repeated Uzi's gesture and stood milk-skinned in the waning moonlight, pantless also, begging me to take her. But my mind was too full of Ziz's words, which I had to keep repeating, so as not to forget them. Thus I turned my back upon my wife and locked myself in the study where, dizzy with slivovitz, I tried to re-create the peculiarities of Ziz's voice.

"Why didn't Stalin make you disappear?" I had asked.

"Because I am a fighter," Ziz had replied. "Poles expect nothing less of their poets."

"That wouldn't have stopped him," I protested.

"Perhaps what people say is true," Ziz said. "Maybe Stalin really believed that I had second sight, that I could put the evil eye on him. Listen, my good friend, we are sitting here enjoying each other like civilized people, but I cannot escape the feeling that I am going to get you into trouble or, the other way round, that you are bringing trouble to me. It is a foolish thought, no?"

He should have asked my wife. "No wonder your body has turned into a fucking notebook," she cried, trying to kick down my door, "you'll be coming ink next!"

My wife was referring, I should explain, to an extraordinary dermatological condition, hives with knobs on, that had developed about the time I got the job on the *Jewish Voice*. The doctor, naming it dermagraphia, had pronounced it psychosomatic — hardly a surprise. At first we treated the welts as a joke. Lena's fingernails became the scalpels that raised vicious scars on my cheeks, making it seem that I had been embracing death by the sword rather than my wife. Smiling her secret smile she wrote obscene messages on my front and love letters behind my back, all of which faded within the hour. But after a while this hypersensitive — nay, hysterical — reaction to passionate physical contact began to worry me. I felt that I had become the unwilling embodiment of my newspaper:

allergic to life, over-sensitive to anti-Semitism. But for history read histamine. While Ziz turns the evil eye upon his torturers I break out in welts. Some hero!

Still, I am something of a hero when the poem appears in the *Jewish Voice*, accompanied by my impersonation of Ziz. "There are times," he is quoted as saying, "when I wish I were a Jew, because there are circumstances in which every honourable man would wish to be one, even if he is dishonest, which is what the first person who recognized my talent was. 'My profession is supposed to be secret,' he told me, 'but everyone knows I am Abe Ratskin the Smuggler. The world must also know you are a poet! Never hide your light under a bushel. But when you show your light, make sure it shines brightly.' This was good advice."

I am a hero to everyone, that is, except Ziz's publisher. His letter arrives stamped: *Without Prejudice*. "Are you crazy?" he wrote. "Do you realize what you've done? Ziz tells me that he gave you the poem 'General Moczar Sings the Blues' as a gift for your wife, not for publication in the *Jewish Voice*. Of all places! Unauthorized publication in the West is illegal, as you must know. By printing the poem you have made it seem that Ziz is deliberately flouting Polish law. Indeed, I have had some indication, which I am not going to vouchsafe to you, that there have already been repercussions. Whether there will be any for you I have yet to decide." As if it were up to him!

"Don't worry," says the editor, proving beyond doubt the paper's need for an astrologer. "I believe you, if only because the Poles have short memories when it comes to Jews. Write down your side of the story and that'll be the end of it."

Of course it is just the beginning. Observe, for almost the last time, the literary editor in his innocence. There he sits — writing the truth! The editor nods, convinced.

"Actually there's something else I want to talk to you about," he says. "The pubs are open, let's do it over a drink."

"Can't tonight, I'm babysitting," I say. "It's my wife's yoga class."

Uzi, suddenly my bosom buddy, also reassures me. "Ziz is just protecting himself," he says. "Fancy a drink?"

"Not tonight," I say.

"Lena's yoga lesson," he says, "I'd forgotten."

7

We meet, a few days later, at the Grosvenor Hotel opposite Hyde Park.

"This is confidential," whispers Uzi. "Don't tell a soul, not even your wife. Ziz wants an invitation to Israel. It can't come from an official body, of course, which rules me out. I thought you might know some literary personage who could issue one."

Thereafter we meet often, clandestinely, like lovers quietly discussing the progress of an affair. It is a charade, this counterfeit adultery, but it makes intimate friends of us within a few weeks.

So much so that it comes as no surprise when Uzi asks, "Do you love your wife?"

"After a fashion," I reply.

"I understand," he says. "In your job you must have many temptations, many affairs."

"None at all," I reply, somewhat shamefacedly, given Uzi's reputation. Indeed, he seems rather disappointed by my answer.

"Do you ever have recurring dreams?" he asks.

I shake my head.

"I do," he says, "I keep dreaming that my nose has turned into a penis. Actually, it's a sensational experience. Imagine fucking a woman and getting a blow job at the same time! Believe me, it's something of a let-down when I wake up with a normal conk. On the other hand, it's a blessing. My wife wouldn't need a shrink to explain the significance of the extra shlong."

"Surely she knows that you betray her," I say.

Dermagraphia

"It's worse than that this time," he says, "I've fallen in love."

"Am I acquainted with the lucky woman?" I ask.

"Not half as well as me," replies Uzi. "Fucking her is so good I think I must be dreaming; which means, of course, that I'm terrified my nose really will turn into a prick."

On the way to our next meeting a dusky beauty puts her hand upon my arm in the lobby of the Grosvenor and addresses me in Hebrew, a language I have not studied since the age of thirteen, though I do know enough to understand, *"Efor Uzi?"*

I try to explain that I am on my way to him and invite her to accompany me, but she refuses, leading me to the assumption that she must be Uzi's magenta-haired siren, no doubt a woman of some standing herself, who would rather not be seen with her lover in so public a place as a hotel bar.

I gather that she would prefer to chat with Uzi on the street. So when I find him half-dozing over his cognac in a velvet armchair I shake him and say, "The woman you love is waiting outside."

Uzi looks at me in utter astonishment. "So you know," he says.

"I'm not a fool," I say, following him through the revolving door.

"Well," says Uzi, once we are on the pavement, "where is she?"

"There," I say, pointing through the pouring rain toward his Mid-Eastern *femme fatale.*

She points back, the way my son does when he is playing Cowboys and Indians. Only her gun is for real. Uzi turns and stares at me as if he thought I had set the trap myself.

"You cunning bastard," he says. His last words before expression of all kind becomes impossible.

A single dumdum bullet hits him in the face. His hands drop. Then the rest of him. While his scalp takes off, showering gobbets of blood, bone, flesh and brain upon

59

Park Lane's pedestrians, who are, luckily, protected by their umbrellas.

Later it transpires that Uzi was shot in error, having been mistaken for the Ambassador himself. None the less, his assassination provides excuse enough for the Israeli government to proceed with the invasion of Lebanon.

"We will cut off the hands of our enemies," vows the Prime Minister. And he sets out in his Biblical way, though using the most modern ballistics, to inflict the original dermagraphic sign, the mark of Cain, upon the face of Lebanon.

In the same week a secret bomb factory in South London blows up, damaging the occupants beyond repair, including Uzi's assassin. Among the charred papers in the hide-out the police find a hit list. Top is the Israeli Ambassador, of course; second is the editor of the *Jewish Voice*, ahead of the chairman of Marks & Spencer.

As a result the Special Branch send an officer along to the newspaper to advise us on security. He seems to enjoy our discomfort, especially mine.

"Jacob," he says, "if I may use your Christian name, the fact is that letter-bombs come in the same packets as books. And we'd hate for you to get blown up instead of the editor."

Hitherto I had got a little thrill from opening the Jiffy bags in the privacy of my office, greedily ripping apart the yellow skin to reveal, amid a cloud of grey matter, the touch of genius within. Now, however, I finger the packages more circumspectly, as if dealing with a lunatic in a padded cell. Being a critic, I am, as you can imagine, well acquainted with the metaphorical language used to sell fiction, as in "this explosive novel", but I have no desire to be present when the metaphor becomes real. I am no surrealist.

But what else was Uzi's death if not surrealistic? To say otherwise would be to admit the full horror of the moment, its reality, and my part in it, which I want to forget. You see, after the girl fired the fatal shot, I began to laugh as if the whole thing were a joke, some farcical by-product of Uzi's philandering. My reaction probably saved my life; after all, it's a bit incongruous, even redundant, to shoot someone who is already laughing his head off.

My wife, however, broke down on hearing the news. She blamed me, as if I could have done anything; then she blamed herself, as if she were somehow responsible.

"It has nothing to do with personalities," I said, "it's history."

Then I remembered Ziz and the evil eye and how Stalin feared him on account of it. My mother, a more benign dictator, also lives in dread of the evil eye, never forgetting *"kayn aynhoreh"* whenever the future tense is introduced. Consequently my son now believes that his full name is *Joshua Kayn Aynhoreh!*

"See," I shout, "you're already screwing him up."

"All you know is to mock," she says. "If they gave degrees for mockery you'd be a Ph.D."

But what if the peasant who spits three times knows more than the professor who seeks rationality in the madhouse of history? Perhaps it really is a matter of placating the right gods, and God help you if you fail. All poor Uzi wanted was to prevent his guilty conscience from going public. And yet this comic cuckolder has suddenly become a character of historical moment, a *causus belli*, for reasons not of personality but of nationality. In other words, while he was busy worrying about his personal behaviour, strangers had judged him as part of a group, found him guilty, sentenced him to death; thereby, in the long run, saving his marriage. In which case it would seem that the manners of an individual are of no consequence, unless you happen to be a despot; and those, it seems, are guided not by a belief in some higher order but by superstition.

Yes, history is whimsical, making stars of the oddest people, who inevitably misinterpret their unexpected prominence. As Old Maxie would put it: we all secretly believe that we deserve what we get.

8

In the main I get letters. These, as a rule, come from sincere ladies of middle age who, having already reviewed for the *Jerusalem Post*, want to write for the *Jewish Voice*. The men tend to be gruffer, older, still bearing grudges left over from literary quarrels with the dead of Mitteleurope. Sometimes I invite the women along to see me, on the off-chance that one or other might be both desirable and adventurous, though Heaven knows what I would do if she were. Anyway, at least two or three times a week I stand chatting with Asa Dorfman, awaiting a visitor.

Since Uzi's assassination and the subsequent discovery of the hit list it is no longer possible to wander off the street into the offices of the *Jewish Voice*. For, on the recommendation of the man from the Special Branch, the swing doors at the front of the building have been ripped out and replaced with ones made of bullet-proof glass. Further, to prevent terrorists from taking aim with their Kalashnikovs, they appear opaque from without, reflecting the street and the outsiders therein, thus turning murder into suicide. At the very least, anyone entering the *Jewish Voice* feels as though they were stepping through the looking-glass.

Once Asa has admitted them and they have signed the Visitors' Book, I introduce myself, despising the disappointment afforded by their spinsterhood. They enthuse over Virginia Woolf or the Women's Movement, and in return I give them an insignificant work to comment upon. Behind their backs, as they depart, Asa Dorfman looks at me and grimaces. Sometimes they turn up unexpectedly, whereupon Asa picks up his phone and snaps, "There's a Miss So-and-So waiting for you down here. Do you want to collect her?"

Thus Miss X finds her way to my office. I have never been over-endowed with social ease, so I am nonplussed when I inspire nerves in others, and Miss X is definitely not comfortable.

Dermagraphia

"Mr Literary Editor," she says, "I believe you already know something about me. But please, I beg you, take no notice of the slanders that certain people are spreading about my character. I know that many so-called academics are as touchy as Freemasons when an interested party begins to question their competence as guardians of holy secrets. And that, Mr Literary Editor, is exactly what I am doing. You probably know that I have just recovered from a breakdown, a recovery I owe to the wonderful editor of the *Jewish Monthly* who bravely published one of my articles. Here is another." She hands me an essay, neatly typed, which maintains with the straightest of faces that Isaac Bashevis Singer is not only a misanthrope and a misogynist but also a homosexual.

Therefore when Asa Dorfman informs me that a Mrs Ben-Tur has turned up in reception my heart does not sing. However, Mrs Ben-Tur proves to be something else. For a start, she has Asa Dorfman eating out of her hand, a phenomenon hitherto unknown. She shakes mine.

"Forgive this intrusion," she says, "but when I saw your interview with Ziz I had to come. You see, although I am now Mrs Ben-Tur, I was formerly Hannah Ratskin. In plain English, Abe Ratskin was my grandfather, whom I never knew. I should love to learn more about him. Would it be too much to ask you to give my address to Ziz? Perhaps he could pass it on to any surviving Ratskins in Poland. I can't write to him directly because I live in Israel. A letter from that destination may do him harm, don't you think?"

"Please," I say, "come up to my office." As she bends to sign her name, Asa Dorfman winks at me.

"Was that your wife?" Old Maxie asks after she has gone.

"No," I say.

"Someone else's wife then," he says.

"I wish I knew someone who had a wife like that," says Meir the Printer.

At last, something the three can agree upon! The desirability of Hannah Ben-Tur.

Her presence haunts my office for days, despite Rabbi

Nathan's intervention. Long since retired, the venerable Rabbi Nathan has become a veritable bibliophile with a hint of kleptomania. Once a month he turns up unembarrassed, confident that the unwritten past no longer exists, to collect all the Hebrew and Yiddish books that have accumulated. No money changes hands, instead I am rewarded with a story.

Today he tells how he performed an exorcism at the Hospital for Jewish Women, an institution in the East End now utilized by later immigrants. Despite this, it was generally agreed that the unquiet shade which stalked the darker wards after midnight was Jewish.

"Not many rabbis were prepared to go, but I had no objections," says mine. "Listen, in Stashev, where I came from, there was a man who became convinced that he had a piece of liver hanging from his ear. All the doctors told him to clear off. Except one. He listened to the man, who was growing desperate by then. You know what he did? After ascertaining whether it was calf's or chicken's liver, the doctor rushed to the butcher's, where he picked up a nice piece. He went home, got his scalpel, ordered the man not to look, and sliced. When the patient turned round he saw the liver in the doctor's hand and was cured. So I said a few prayers in the hospital. I am a rationalist. But what harm? The nurses were very grateful." He repeats the prayers, for my benefit; but Hannah Ben-Tur won't go away, nor will the ghost of Uzi, who whispers, "Remember my nose."

9

Rabbi Nathan is not the only kleptomaniac on the premises, however, for someone else has begun to spirit books away from my office. It gets so bad that I am forced to take the most expensive volumes home with me, much to the delight of my little boy, who sits upon my lap and demands "stories".

But my wife, somewhat regretful over her lapsed career and rather more resentful in her new role of housekeeper,

Dermagraphia

complains that all the rooms are being overrun by books.

"If it wasn't for books," I say, "you wouldn't get invited to glamorous affairs like Uzi's party for Ziz."

"Big deal," she says. "Since then I haven't been able to look any of your literary friends in the face. Not that they're looking at my face anyway."

"Don't be such a spoilsport," I say. "If it's any compensation, I found the evening an inspiration. You know my stories come from finding unexpected connections. Like those word games in which you had to turn 'book' into 'bomb' in two moves. Well, your boobs made the connection."

"You didn't mind?" she says.

"What?" I ask.

"That the whole of London saw my tits," she says.

"No," I say.

"You weren't jealous?" she asks.

"Certainly not," I say, "it was a turn-on."

"You didn't show it," she says.

"Business before pleasure," I say.

"So I'm not just a drudge?" she says.

"Why do you say that?" I ask.

"Because I feel like one," she replies.

"That's crazy," I say.

"What do you know?" she says. "I used to be a teacher and that, believe it or not, gave me a sense of identity. Now I run about all day after Josh — who is wonderful, but you try it day after day — and I cook for you. Tell me, what do I do for myself? Am I anything more than Josh's mother and your bottle-washer? OK, that I'll be. But I'm not cleaning the house as well."

"I'll help," I say.

"You make the bed once a week," she says. "It's not enough."

"If I did any more," I say, "I wouldn't have time to write."

"I know," she says.

"So what do you want?" I ask.

65

"A servant," she replies.

A week later Mrs Swallow begins work. My wife, somewhat uncomfortable, keeps getting in the way.

"Don't worry, deary," says Mrs Swallow, a cheery soul, but not insensitive, "if I didn't have busy hands I'd be a busybody. And you can't live by words alone."

"Tell that to my husband," says my wife, who subsequently accuses the same of stealing her silk panties.

"Why should I want them?" I ask.

"Because you're perverted," says my wife, "or perhaps you have a mistress with a constant need for bonbons."

I wonder, briefly, why she was looking for them in the first place. The following day she apologizes.

"I watched her do it," she adds.

"Who? What?" I ask.

"Mrs Swallow," she says, "going through my undies."

"She'd never get into them," I observe.

"Nevertheless," replies my wife, "I saw her stuff my sexy cami-knickers into her apron."

"Bloody cheek," I say. "Have you given her the sack?"

"Of course not," says my wife, "the house has never been cleaner."

It is a miserable summer, despite Mrs Swallow. Uzi was shot in June. By September I am getting dermagraphia merely from touching newspapers. As a child the very sound of "beetroot" was enough to induce nausea, now "Beirut" has the same effect. So, sick and itchy, I kiss my equally irritable wife and make my way to the *Jewish Voice* where Old Maxie — bloody cheek — complains that my book reviews are too recondite.

"There's an old Jewish joke," he says, "the punchline of which goes something like this: 'If I knew what's what, I wouldn't be here now.' Well, our readers want to know what's what; they aren't interested in the introspections of your pseudo-intellectual friends. I'll tell you the trouble with intellectuals for nothing. Despite all your pretence, you're really more concerned with who's who than what's what."

Dermagraphia

I repeat this to Meir the Printer.

"You should remind the postman," he says with a smile, "that the battle-cry of the pogromniks in Tsarist Russia was *Daloy gramotniye*, which means 'Down with the intellectuals'."

10

And so the days pass, piling gloom upon gloom. At home only little Joshua remains cheerful. And Mrs Swallow, our ill-named magpie, who hands me the morning's post. Rubbish. Rubbish. What's this? A letter from Ziz!

"My dear friend," he writes, "I cannot begin to say how sorry I was about the death of our mutual companion. That such a thing should happen in England! The response of his government is no more fortunate, however, for it has made an impossibility of my mission. But before I return to Poland I should consider it a privilege to spend an evening in the company of yourself and your most beautiful wife. . . ."

Of whom I have had enough.

Instead I telephone the hotel of Hannah Ben-Tur, in the hope that she also is still in England. Heaven be praised!

"I have arranged a meeting with Ziz," I say. "You'll never get a better chance to enquire about your grandfather."

"Why, Mr Silkstone," says Hannah Ben-Tur (née Ratskin), "you are a magician."

"My friend," says Ziz as he opens the door of his seedy rented apartment in Belsize Park, "not only do you have a beautiful wife, but you have an even more splendid mistress. I am prepared to offer you the secret of my poetry in exchange for your love potion."

"Actually," I say, "this is Hannah Ben-Tur, happily married mother of four, and granddaughter of your old guide, Abe Ratskin."

"There was a man," sighs Ziz. "Come in, come in. Please. We will talk."

The lounge, to which Ziz leads us, looks as if a nomadic tribe had made it their headquarters. Cushions litter the floor, upon which empty bottles roll like recently deceased skittles, while the tables are stacked with papers, books, coffee cups and over-stocked ashtrays. The room is illuminated by a bright, bare bulb which flatters neither it nor me.

"Jacob," cries Ziz, "what is wrong with your face? You look like you have duelled with every student in Heidelberg!"

"I am allergic to Jews," I say, "in particular their history."

"You should have met Abe Ratskin," he says, "but even he, a prince among men, died of inner bleeding. Too much of this," he adds, pointing to a fresh bottle of Wyborowa. "Our own internal fire-water, not the watered-down stuff we export."

"Tell me about Grandpa," says Hannah. Her eyes and her mouth conspire to produce a smile that promises illicit delights in return for such information, from which I deduce that Abe Ratskin's profession has had genetic consequences; Hannah is a smuggler of love.

"My dear lady," says Ziz, "your grandfather was a hero of the Resistance, a carrier of messages and more between the Jews of Podgórze and the underground army outside. Even better, he saved my life. At the time of the German invasion I was still a student at the *Uniwersytet Jagiellonski*, although I had already published my first book of poems. That same November I received an invitation to hear a lecture on the subject of 'The Attitude of the German Authorities to Science and Teaching' in the university hall. Abe pleaded with me not to go, but I was young and foolish and things were not yet too bad. Besides, I was flattered to be among the few students who had been asked. As it turned out, I was more battered than flattered, for the lecture was a pretext. No sooner were we all assembled than the Gestapo burst in and arrested the lot of us. We were all pushed and kicked, including the most

Dermagraphia

distinguished professors in Poland, and bundled into waiting lorries. Then, at the last moment, the soldier who was supposed to have locked us in whispered, 'Run for your lives. I will shoot, but do not be alarmed, the bullets will go over your heads.' I didn't hesitate. I jumped. But I ran alone. The others were too shocked or too old. The soldier was as good as his word. Later I learned that he had been bribed by Abe Ratskin. With what? Money? Alcohol? Women? All three probably. My dear, I would have gone to Germany and shot Hitler himself if old Abe had promised me a kiss from his granddaughter."

So Hannah, having drunk her share of the vodka, crosses the room and kisses the great poet upon the lips. That done, she sits upon his lap.

"We are, in a manner of speaking, brother and sister," says Ziz, "for Abe Ratskin gave us both life. Otherwise I would beg you to stay the night. But I am too good a Catholic and incest is too strong a taboo. As it is, I must leave you in the good hands of my great friend, the literary editor of the *Jewish Voice*."

Hannah giggles and hugs her new-found relative. "I have never seen a photograph of Grandpa," she says. "What did he look like?"

"Let me tell you," says Ziz. "Whenever I see your Minister of Defence on the television I feel shivers all over. He is your grandfather's *doppelgänger*."

The bottle of vodka empties like an egg-timer, signifying the end of the evening.

"I have a leaving present for you," says Ziz. "A Polish joke. A friend of mine, a Jew, was accused of bringing up his children in a religious atmosphere. He was denounced as a hypocrite and expelled from the Party. Finally, given a chance to speak, he protested that he didn't actually have any children. Whereupon the committee upheld the expulsion on account of his provocative silence. The moral, my children, is simple: you may as well be hung for a sheep as a lamb."

As we stroll back to the car Hannah puts her arm through

69

mine, clinging so tightly that her left breast makes contact and sends sense data direct to my brain, enabling me to produce a contour map of the said gland which, like all delightful scenery, excites the desire for further exploration. My mind, being fuddled, finds everything in the automobile an innuendo for pudenda or phallus, and this is not even taking into account Hannah's obvious invitation to touch the real thing. Thus the drive back to the hotel is a triumph of the straight and narrow over the crooked and the devious; we could easily have crashed or fucked but, in the event, we do neither and arrive safely.

"Will you come up?" asks Hannah.

"OK," I say, "for twenty minutes."

"I'd prefer an hour for the first time, wouldn't you?" she says.

As we ascend in the lift, arm in arm, Hannah murmurs: "You're amazing, Mr Silkstone. I can say whatever comes into my head and you don't bat an eyelid. There's a double-bed in my room, you know."

As if I didn't! Once inside, Hannah stands so close that we look, in outline, like some unambiguous creature with two backs, joined, of course, at the genitals.

"I've dropped enough hints," she whispers, "for you to grasp that I am not a prick-teaser. It's up to you."

"Aren't you happily married?" I ask.

"I'm thirty-four," she replies. "I've decided to start being happily married when I reach thirty-five."

Tongue-tied, I kiss her, because I cannot help myself, but also because I cannot bring myself to utter the words that will make the betrayal of my wife inevitable.

However, it is not for reasons of conscience that I dally; no, it is superstition that holds me back. I am convinced that as selfish an act as adultery will occasion Job-like punishment to be visited, not upon me, but upon my wife or child. And such responsibility is beyond me. Here I am, a twentieth-century man in a post-religious society with my tongue in the mouth of another man's wife and a weeping cyclops in my pants, but also with a medieval dread of developing the evil eye.

So strong is the fear that I am suddenly seized by a compulsion to telephone my wife lest, unknown to me, some calamity has overtaken my family. This obsession is easily the equal of my passion for Hannah which, God knows, is real enough. Meanwhile Hannah, anxious to accelerate the sticking point, bites me on the neck, and is astonished at the immediate result.

"I feel like a vampire," she says.

"It makes infidelity a little difficult," I say, "when your wife can read you like a book."

"It's an excuse," snaps Hannah, "a psychosomatic excuse. You're frightened of being touched by reality."

"We'll see," I say. "Have lunch with me tomorrow."

11

To my amazement Hannah turns up. In the meantime, recalling Ziz's final words, a benediction upon our coupling, I have been regretting my lost opportunity. Rather, I have been rewriting history. What if I had said, "Yes, let's do it, now!" — what if I had undone Hannah Ben-Tur, stripped her down to her bare flesh, fallen upon her breasts, rammed my penis into her belly? What if we had loosened every restraint and forsaken all others for the sake of ourselves? Would anything be different? Of course not!

Then Uzi whispers, "Remember me."

"Your death had nothing to do with you," I hiss.

"Suit yourself," he says.

To take my mind off my obsessive revisionism, I sit down to type out a review I want to get into next week's paper. My father, ex-member of the furniture trade, had written, at my request, a moving little meditation in long-hand upon the diary of an ordinary cabinet-maker, published by his local museum. "I have vivid recollections of my elder brother wheeling a barrow-full of solid oak bureaus from our workshop to the nearby french polishers," I transcribe, "and I can remember the smell of the glue being slowly heated in an iron pot over a gas ring, the fine coating of sawdust which permeated every corner of the workshop, and the ever-present problem of disposing of the bags of wood shavings which were heaped in a corner." Me too! Back come the aromas of long-gone Saturdays when he took me to the much grander factory in Arlington Avenue he owned with his brothers, where I would be treated like a little lord by the workmen, because I was the son of the boss, whom everyone called Dave.

But then Asa Dorfman informs me that Mrs Ben-Tur is back again, and the ancestral voices are replaced by the insinuating nudge of a tempter. "Don't let history repeat itself," it says, "learn from your mistakes."

At least I have learned one thing: how my wife feels, living for others. In particular, the frustration. Which is what I experience, sure enough, when I go down to meet Hannah. Abe Dorfman, Old Maxie and Meir the Printer all give knowing looks as I escort her to my office.

Hannah, thoughtfully, has brought a picnic: golden apples, honey sandwiches and Smirnoff vodka. I pour the drinks.

"How much do you want?" I ask.

"A lot," she replies.

I comply.

"Look at me," says Hannah. "I'm in the heart of the *tsuris* industry and I haven't got a care in the world."

"You're lucky," I reply.

"That's what is so wonderful about Israel," she says. "Everywhere else seems unbelievably pacific by comparison. How's your dermagraphia?"

"All clear," I say.

"Let me see," she says, "unbutton your shirt."

Mindlessly I oblige.

"Nice," she says. Before I can step aside she rakes her fingers down my stomach, raising immediate welts. "You're going to get into trouble with your wife anyway,"

Dermagraphia

she says, "so you may as well commit what you're going to be accused of."

"Here?" I say. "In the office?"

"Why not?" she says. "Lock the door."

"There's no key," I say. "As for the walls . . . not only do they have ears, they've got tongues as well."

"And do you have eyes?" asks Hannah, as she steps out of her dress.

Incongruity can sometimes make things seem absurd, but Hannah's bravado has imparted an erotic charge that is impossible to evade.

"Touch my breasts," she says.

And I do.

"Now we're getting somewhere," she says, as I slip my hand down the front of her pants.

Hannah, for her part, unbuckles my belt and unfastens my jeans, making room for her hand to reciprocate. Having assured herself of my willingness to participate and rubbed a little man-made lubrication on her finger, she encircles my middle and shoves the slippery digit into my anus, causing me to groan aloud, though with pleasure or pain I am not certain.

With her finger thus, in the grip of my sphincters, Hannah whispers: "Why, Mr Silkstone, you don't seem to want to let me go."

I look around the office, as if for the last time, taking in the books and the cluttered desk and the unfinished page in my typewriter. My final thoughts, before I give myself up completely to Hannah's more powerful desires, concern my father's heartbroken look as I casually mention that I am leaving Lena and his grandson.

"How could you?" he cries.

"Take a look at Hannah for yourself," I reply, "how could I not?"

At which point Old Maxie, the office postman, enters with a delivery of books.

"Excuse me," he says.

"Fuck," I say.

73

"Not today, it seems," says Hannah Ben-Tur (*née* Ratskin), who decides to spend Rosh Hashana with her family.

12

I sit glumly in my office all afternoon, not daring to go home before I've had a word with Old Maxie, dreading what my wife will say when I do. How can I explain away the welts on my chest? And what improbable excuse can I find for having my hand in the pants of an otherwise naked woman, not to mention vice versa?

Old Maxie eventually turns up, as I knew he would. This time he knocks with mock servility.

"You are a lucky man, Mr Silkstone," he says. "Mrs Ben-Tur undoubtedly has a beautiful body. But you are also a foolish one. The *Jewish Voice* is well named. There are no secrets in this building. Everything is revealed in the end. So I am going to tell you mine. I am the person who has been removing the books from your office. I started after you asked Meir the Printer to translate Ziz's poem instead of me. Do you have any idea how hurtful that was? Books are my life, Mr Silkstone, more than they are yours. I have no wife to betray. I am telling you this now because you are helpless. But I am not vindictive. I will sell you my silence. Not for money, but for books. I want first refusal on everything that comes in."

"How about the ones I need for review?" I ask.

"You'll just have to go to a shop and buy a second copy," he replies.

I have no choice, of course, but this once, to spite him, I stuff my briefcase with the day's unopened Jiffy bags.

My little boy is looking out of the window when I return home.

"Daddy," he cries, spotting the packages, "have you brought me a present?"

"You can see tomorrow," says my wife. "It's time for bed now. I've got to talk to Daddy." *Oh, God,* I think, *does she*

Dermagraphia

know already? Am I that transparent? Or has Old Maxie phoned her?

"Can Daddy read to me?" asks Joshua.

"Of course," I say. For once I pray for him to keep his eyes open as I recite his favourite nursery rhymes, but he obstinately drops off, leaving me with no alternative but to face the consequences.

Downstairs, as expected, my wife is crying.

"I'm sorry," I say.

"You're sorry!" she screams. "I wish I'd never been born!"

"Nothing really happened," I say.

"What do you know, you fool?" she hisses. "Of course it did. I was Uzi's mistress. We made love every week. From the night of the party until he was shot."

"How?" I ask. Relieved, initially, that I have been let off the hook, then suddenly sick with shock.

"When you thought I was at yoga," she replies.

"Why tonight?" I ask.

"Because the guilt was strangling me," she answers.

"Perhaps I will instead," I say.

"I doubt it," she says.

What a joke! What a reward for my fidelity!

"There's more," says my wife. "I've also been sleeping with Ziz."

"What?!" I cry. Ziz? The good Catholic!

"One night Uzi couldn't make it. In fact he had to go to dinner with your editor," continues my wife. "Anyway, Ziz was waiting for me instead. He knew all about my affair with Uzi. 'My little diplomatic triumph', he called it. You see, Ziz was the one who persuaded Uzi to pursue me." I might have guessed! "He was irresistible." The two-faced swine! No wonder he wanted me to have Hannah!

"I'm surprised the old goat could still get it up," I say.

"He managed all right," says my wife, wanting to hurt, "with a little help. He liked me to wear sexy undies." Lena senses she may have gone too far. "I'm sorry," she says.

"Fuck off," I say.

75

"Damn you," she says, "I refuse to make excuses or ask forgiveness. It happened and it is over. There's no reason why anyone should be any the worse for it."

Except Uzi, I think, now sadly defaced.

"It may even do us some good," she adds, "perhaps you'll appreciate me a bit more. Well, say something."

I'll tell you what I'm thinking: *I wish I'd fucked Hannah Ben-Tur to within an inch of her life.* Idiot that I was.

"Did Uzi make you come?" I ask. "Was he as good as his boasts?"

"Is that all you can think of?" she says.

"Yes," I reply.

"You're a bastard," she says.

"And you're a whore," I reply. OK, I confess, I'm a hypocrite, for which I am punished.

As if to say "I told you so" my over-active mind afflicts my body with ferocious hives, Uzi's legacy.

"Can't you stop fidgeting?" moans my wife in her otherwise undisturbed slumber.

But my body won't let me alone. I am too weak to resist the imperative to scratch, but self-possessed enough to know that such five-fingered frenzy will only make matters worse. The best I can do is impose some order upon my volcanic inspiration.

Disturbing Lena as little as possible I remove an empty fountain pen (a bar-mitzvah present) from my desk and begin to write upon the crawling parchment that covers my bones. Thanks to this legerdemain the hives are quickly forgotten as dermagraphia transforms the invisible ink into legible inscriptions. Above my groin is written: "The king," over my heart: "A stone," across my belly: "Appetite is all," on my forehead: "Make me mindless," et cetera. I am a dissident writer! I am Ziz! The Thought Police no longer scare me. Who needs them when we are quite capable of torturing ourselves?

But this bravado does not last and by morning my volatile words have vanished. Words on paper last longer, but their destiny is the same. God knows why dictators fear

Dermagraphia

us. Writers are only dangers to themselves.

Glad to be out of my nettle-bed I leave for the office before anyone else is even awake. I open my mail, proof-read the articles back from the printer and, aided by a typographer, lay out next week's Books Page, balancing the nepotism with an eccentric review of the new Singer by Miss X.

Old Maxie comes in about lunch-time to check if there are any books and I shake my head and smile inwardly at my gulling of this bibliolatrous blackmailer. Just as I am picturing the inviolate Jiffy bags sitting upon my desk, the telephone rings. The voice at the other end is so hysterical that, at first, I don't recognize my wife.

"Murderer!" she screams. "Murderer!"

"Who's that?" I say.

"You wanted to kill me!" she cries.

"You're crazy," I say.

"That's why you left those parcels behind," she says. "Well, it wasn't me you got. May God forgive you!"

"Who?" I yell. But she has cut me off. *Dear God, I pray, don't let it be Josh. Not him!*

"Where's the fire?" asks Old Maxie as I push him out of the way.

Sure enough, the otherwise placid air around our house is being whipped by the rotating blue lights of ambulances, fire engines and police cars flagellating my soul also — being no Abraham, nor even a Ziz, but only the accidental murderer of my son. Frantically I look among the crowds, who shake their heads among themselves as if unwilling to give voice to the bad news in their hearts. Where is my wife? At last I spot her amid a group of detectives. But I can only see her back.

Then she turns and there, in her arms, is Joshua, *kayn aynhoreh*. But why so blue in the face? The lights, the lights. Of course.

"That's him," screams Lena, "that's the man you want!"

Hang on, I think, *I'm innocent. You're the one who was prepared to sacrifice your family.*

"What happened?" I ask.

"My present went boom," says Joshua, "I was a bit frightened."

"Mrs Swallow started to unpack the books for him," says my wife. "You can guess the rest. Her hands were blown off. Both of them."

I can't help myself. I burst out laughing. Poor Mrs Swallow.

III   In England's Green and
       Pleasant Land

1

The viridescent meadow is polka-dotted with dandelions as if suffering from a yellow pox. In fact its frazzled grass has been sprayed with green panel-paint filched from a local garage by the Children of Albion, a number of whom even now wander across the sward in snakeskin boots and surgical masks, applying the finishing touches. Some droplets spiral upwards on the evening zephyrs attracting golden-knops with the false promise of an aphid glut. These draw the swifts, who swoop upon the ladybirds, but are disappointed in turn by their bitter taste.

The same breezes ruffle the tight-bodiced polonaises on the chic peasants, which split to reveal their own man traps. Such sights are lost on the mistletoe berries that stare blindly out of a zinc tub at the limbs that are about to crush them. Unselfconsciously knotting the skirts around their waists, these merciless women stamp out the last drop of viscin from the druidical aphrodisiac that even so is tempting me to kiss their shiny legs. Alchemists in wizard waistcoasts then transform the resulting goo into bird-lime, which they brush on to the branches of the acorn-encrusted oaks and the corpses of elms.

Finally, as the sun begins to sink, turning the jagged stubble in the adjoining fields into gilded teeth, a jester wags his wineskin at a group of jerkin-clad serfs who proceed to raise a huge canvas at the entrance to the meadow, imposing a dream landscape between us and reality. Now, instead of the flat arable lands with their livery soil, we see two mountain ranges. At the vanishing point where they meet, the unknown artist has painted a huge sun whose luminosity penetrates the valley on shafts of light. Dead centre is the pathway to enlightenment, the beginning of which will be the entrance to the Fair.

At present in that gateway between the quotidian and

the other world a faun-like individual sits upon a bale of straw, playing the pipes of Pan while the menials secure the canvas with guy-ropes and tent-pegs lest it vanish like a mirage. Likewise, even these ethereal beings have to eat and when we observe a pubescent Daughter of Albion lead a sedated freemartin toward a butcher's block we look at our own boy and decide that the ensuing banquet, despite the collective name of the diners, will hardly be *virginibus puerisque*.

2

Do they know, these animated figments of the Anglo-Saxon unconscious, that beneath their feet is real history? For I have seen their tarted-up meadow stripped bare and the hitherto unsuspected Roman settlement revealed. If you consult the report of the 1980-81 seasons, published by the Kingsland Archaeological Association, you will see listed among those volunteers who made the excavation work possible with their enthusiasm and cheerful effort the names of Jake and Lena Silkstone.

3

The first woman I ever desired, long before I married Lena, was my history teacher at St Martin's. I was nine or ten, she was in full bloom. But it wasn't for her looks that I loved her, but for her stories — that's what history was in those days. Never will I forget the day she took her favourite class to Westminster Bridge. There we stood open-mouthed beneath the ravishing statue of Queen Boudicca while Miss Lewis told us the details of her heroic life and tragic death. No wonder Miss Lewis always looked so sad.

Fighting back the tears, she began: "When old King Prasutagus was dying, he named wicked Nero as his heir, thereby hoping to secure a portion of his lands for his two daughters. But no sooner was he dead than the Emperor seized the lot. Beautiful queen Boudicca (who was much younger than her husband) was furious. Children, I hardly dare tell you with what cruelty the Romans received her. Orders were given that she should be publicly whipped and her daughters exposed to the brutality of the soldiers. They were obeyed."

I can still picture the scene as vividly as if I had been a blue-faced Iceni forced to witness the humiliation of his queen. Wearing nothing but a coarse-spun shift she was dragged by her hair to the crude stocks where her husband had the riff-raff flogged. There she was pushed to her knees. The gods were merciful; her back was to me so I could not see her face. It was an icy day; the wind blew straight across the marshes from the sunless lands to the east. Instead of throwing a blanket over my queen, the soldiers exposed her to the elements and my undeserving gaze. Oh, I didn't want to look but I couldn't take my eyes off her opening that, despite itself, was well disposed toward even the meanest beast. Even so no Roman dared touch her in that way, though they mimicked rutting animals behind her back and one, more sacriligious than the rest, crawled beneath her and took a breast in his mouth. However, this mock-Romulus soon ran off when the officers appeared.

No shame was spared my poor queen. Although she withstood the first blows she eventually lost control of herself and moved her bowels. When the whipping was over, she was indeed no better than a four-legged creature. Breathy clouds came from her slack mouth while steam rose from her sweating flanks and her raw back, as well as from the pile of her own excrement.

Still the Romans were not finished with my queen. The officer in charge filled a bowl with slops from a drinking trough and threw the contents in her face. Then he pulled her hair until her head was upright. Thus she was forced to witness the rape of her daughters.

"Where is the pride of the Iceni now?" screamed the officer. "Your next king will be a centurian's bastard!"

No wonder, as Miss Lewis put it, that the Britons, with

Boudicca at their head in her chariot with its famous scythes, took up arms to shake off the Roman yoke. Camulodunum was taken, and Verulamium, where the Silkstones now live, was destroyed. Nor was Kingsland Meadow spared her fiery revenge.

4

These days, of course, I am aware that my past was elsewhere and that if I had joined any revolt against the Romans it would have been Bar Kochba's. But, for the present I am here, reviving the English dead, though I am more used to invention than creation. "Once upon a time," my beginning, "they lived happily ever after" my ending, or variations thereon. I am as a consequence of being a man of letters — don't laugh — something of a progressive carrying a world upon my shoulders into such future as a pessimist can envisage. It's a tiring business, and I'm glad of a rest.

So every weekend, in our halcyon summers of 1980 and '81, we went down to Kingsland Meadow to assist at the dig. How much more pleasant it is to be an archaeologist! They already have the ending and can work backwards from there, finding the connecting images not in their imaginations but in the dirt and slime, if there is any difference. What they can do with spade and trowel, I have to accomplish with my mind, excavating myself while the world's their oyster. No wonder that Adam Smith, the director of the dig, called me "the miserable sod".

Not that he was particularly cheerful himself. A builder by profession, his hobby continually undermined his confidence in his own constructions, underlining their inevitable fate. Moreover, his marriage had recently collapsed, his wife having decided that she was a lesbian. The couple, on their last legs, had repaired to the local vicar, newly ordained.

"Do you know what he asked?" yelled Adam. "Did we like doing it? Did we have any trouble with orgasms, for example? A vicar said that, without a blush! 'No,' replied my wife, 'I've always found the idea of a man on top of me repulsive. Orgasms? What are they? I learned how to fake them at the pictures.' In front of me, after a decade of marriage. The cold-hearted bitch! 'You must follow the dictates of your nature,' he said. God damn him and all other fashionable pricks. Who needs pantheism in the church? I'd rather be a pagan or even a Jew than a fucking Christian. Give me a vengeful God any day. What's the point of marriage vows if the vicar himself tells you it's OK to poke your own kind with fingers or whatever else they use? We'll end up like the Romans, mark my words — fornicating while the barbarians take over.''

Thereafter Adam began fornicating with the local librarian, who shared his passion for the ancient world. Probably to escape from the messy present, they began tramping through local fields in the wake of the plough and were surprised by the number of artefacts they turned up in Kingsland Meadow, including the Belgic brooch his replacement wife now wore. She checked the charts in her library and the local museum and observed that Kingsland Meadow had no signs of occupation marked on it, perhaps because it had not been farmed at the time of the survey. Pretty sure by now that they were dealing with a previously unknown site, they obtained permission from the landowner to commence excavations.

On that first afternoon in May 1979 they discovered, beneath the topsoil and the accumulated debris, the cement floor of a substantial room. Usually spectres haunt solid buildings but that night, after the other helpers had departed, two incarnate beings passed through the invisible walls of the ghostly villa and re-enacted the rudiments of procreation on the uncovered foundations. Raising himself up to give more strength to his final thrust, Adam found the ground giving way beneath his hands. Through the floor they went and into the void below, leaving him helplessly stuck inside his lover.

She eventually wriggled out, grazing back and buttocks

in the process and placing a bloody deposit on the vacant lot. Lifted clear of the lovers' stocks Adam got a torch from their caravan and looked into the larger of the holes, seeing rows of dressed stone columns receding toward infinity.

Shivering slightly, he lowered himself down into the underground maze and crawled along till the air ran out.

"Thereby providing," I replied, "a metaphor for life itself."

"God, you writers," snapped Adam, "It was a hypocaust. Perfectly preserved. Isn't that enough?"

"Jake needs to know the meaning of everything," explained my wife. "He can't bear suspense. That's why he hates uncertainty."

So we sought, in our different ways, to make sense of Kingsland Meadow.

Having uncovered the hypocaust on the first day, Adam refused to get carried away, being a methodical man. He overlaid the meadow with a grid in the manner of Mortimer Wheeler and began excavating each box in turn. Within a few weeks he had uncovered the foundations of eight adjoining rooms. And then a strange thing happened.

Standing within his ruin, the latter-day builder began to fancy himself as a Roman architect surveying not the end but the beginning. The stones, being both, were indifferent to the magic they performed, but we all noticed the change in Adam. No longer a Little Englander, he began praising the glories of Continental culture, exemplified by the Roman occupation.

"Quisling," hissed the librarian.

"They weren't soft, the Romans. Not the colonials at any rate," said Adam, "not like we've become. The Soviets could move in tomorrow. No one would raise a finger. We've become a petty backwater full of nancy-boys and leslies. Your lot, Jake. The Israelis. They're the only ones who know what's what these days. Bar Kochba, Ben-Gurion. Sons of a gun, all of 'em."

"If Bar Kochba, why not Boudicca?" said the librarian. "She also gave the Romans a bloody nose."

"No one's ever accused me of being a philo-Semite," said Adam, "but at least they had a culture to defend. Boudicca was a nihilist. Her followers were no better than football hooligans."

"I think Adam's just scared of assertive women," I added, "especially ones with masculine characteristics."

"You can stick your pseudo-psychiatry up your arse," replied Adam. "It just shows how little you understand. You think that just because I read the *Mail* I'm a crypto-Fascist. Well, I'm not. I am a builder. I have visions of the future, of a new society based upon Roman values."

Nevertheless we went backwards in time, through the various layers of occupation, towards the architect's original conception. In the last room we found, some eighteen inches below the surface, a human skeleton. Adam went white, as if suddenly revealed as the murderer of his wife, but of course the corpse was Roman, so the police returned to their duties elsewhere.

"One of Boudicca's victims?" I enquired.

"Much too late," said Adam.

"Then who was she?"

From the waist down there was nothing, no pelvis to confirm her sex, but the skull (or what was left of it) was typically female. She was, according to her teeth, between twenty-five and thirty. Eternally enigmatic she rested on her front in her last bed, inclined toward the left, her sinister arm flexed, with her hand shielding what was once her face, as if determined even there to evade the paparazzi. Or, vain to the last, did she hold a mirror to observe the life drain from her beautiful features? Certainly her death was not natural, nor was her burial orthodox. We put her remains in a suitcase and gave them to the nearest vicar, but she returned from her recreational jaunt to haunt us.

Twelve inches below her grave we uncovered a tessellated pavement depicting, on the threshold, two dolphins and, in the centre, encircled by a wreath of vine leaves, a bust of Venus — also with her left arm raised. No ambiguity here, the goddess was checking her hair in a mirror. Reddish-brown, it was massed in waves on either side of her head with locks curling over her undraped shoulders. It was as though we were being offered a lesson on the relationship between life and art. First comes art, then life; the latter imitating the former — the mosaic having predicted a situation that was actually re-enacted upon it some two centuries later. For let us suppose that the woman (in a far shabbier room, Venus obscured by rubble) was surprised while regarding herself in a looking-glass — by whom? The mosaic gave no clue. It was a story with a beginning and an end, but no middle. So the question returned. Who was she? *Once upon a time,* I thought, as I began her obituary . . . and knew instantly that my infatuation with archaeology was concluded. It was too much like writing, after all.

5

In the spring of 1982, about the time my wife began fucking the Israeli Cultural Attaché, Adam Smith and his remaining helpers completed their work at Kingsland Meadow. They filled in the excavation, compressed the soil with rollers, sowed grass-seed and departed to finish the book of the dig. At the end of that summer, just as the Children of Israel were preparing to enter Beirut, the Children of Albion took over the meadow for their fair. Having observed their elaborate preparations on the eve of the grand opening, we are curious and return the following day.

Black flecks of charred stubble descend from the saturnine sky as we pay our pennies to the faun at the borderline and enter the enchanted field. Made suspicious by the woodland deity's horns and tail, our little boy asks, "Was he the devil?"

Not without justification, for the meadow looks like an oasis in hell, being surrounded by burning fields. Farm-workers, dimly visible through the smoke, stand with blazing torches daubing the broken stalks with flames, while the farmers mount guard without, shotgun on shoulder, waiting to put the terrified rabbits out of their misery. But louder than summer's fatal rites is the cascade of birdsong that spins a veil between us and the world. Diurnal nightingales, blackbirds and missel-thrushes sit tamely on overhanging branches singing their hearts out. Some of the wilder boys begin to stone them, but even then they do not flock elsewhere. Their wings flutter, but to no avail, as if gravity had suddenly got too much for them, though they do not fall when they are hit.

"Why don't they fly away?" asks our little boy.

"Because they are stuck," I reply, remembering the wizardry of viscid birdlime that has doomed them to harmonious extinction. And panic glues my own feet to the velveteen sheen that covers the turf, convincing me that I have become a component in some exquisitely obscene musical box.

Unwilling to stand still, I lead my family past vegetarian burger stands, spice stalls, portrait painters, cobblers, necromancers, blacksmiths, weavers and wood-workers, past eccentric equestriennes knitting plaits in the tails of their equine lovers, past steam tractors and threshing-machines, masterminded by a strangely compelling cracker-barrel philosopher, until we reach a marquee which seems less salubrious than most.

A seedy barker in tux-trousers, bowler, braces, white tie and no shirt stands on a grubby platform shouting into a loud-hailer, "This is where the naughty girls perform!"

A white whippet with a green garter in place of a collar wees on his plimsolls. "Gents, take a lead from this wimp," he cries, "clear your decks for action!"

Whereupon the pimp kicks the dog out of the way and yells, "Come on, Sharon, show 'em what you've got!"

From the shadows in a black gymslip steps Sharon, who bows with her back to the audience, thereby revealing exactly where her fishnet stockings connect with her suspender belt. Inspired by the concomitant catcalls, the decadent showman flicks up the tail-end of her skirt with his riding-crop and raps her on the buttocks, raising whinnies from Sharon and an atavistic memory from me that I know is as false as her pleasure. For when she turns I see that her face, despite the painted smile, promises revenge.

One, two, three, four more girls appear.

"Now, gents," cries the ringmaster, "you're about to see something even Edward VII never did! The uncensored French cancan. Yes, gents, just fill my hat with silver and the girls will begin the beguine."

"Let's go," says Lena.

"Spoilsport," I reply.

"OK," says Lena, "we'll do a deal. I'll count the hairs on their G-strings if you grant me a wish."

Later, as we take Joshua back to the threshing-machine, for a second time at old-time farming, Lena lingers outside a caravan disconcertingly decorated with swastikas. It belongs to a fortune-teller who obviously failed to predict the outcome of World War II.

"Tit for tat," says Lena, "you made me look up half a dozen cunts. Now it's your turn. I want you to look into the future."

"You know how superstitious I am," I say. "What if she sees something terrible?"

"Chickenshit," Lena replies.

"You really want me to go in," I ask, "even though the woman is obviously a Nazi?"

Lena nods. "I'd like to know if our marriage is going to last," she says.

So I ascend.

6

The first thing I see is a marmoset masturbating upon the shoulder of a virilescent fortune-teller — not exactly my image of the promised future.

"What have we here, my pet?" she (or he) whispers.

"Why, it's a Semitic gentleman. How do I know? I'll tell you a secret: not by your face, but by the Jewish cross on your necklace. Don't let my fylfots bother you; they have nothing to do with the late Adolf Hitler. I worship *science*, not man."

The introduction of that word makes me uncomfortable. I would have preferred tomfoolery, which I could have laughed off. Moreover, there is something uncannily familiar about the indeterminate individual squatting on the three-legged stool who polishes the crystal ball as if it were a piece of laboratory equipment. The beams of light it scatters upon its rotation suddenly bring to mind a Tuesday morning, over twenty years before, when this same character, then our science teacher, carelessly dropped a lump of sodium into a bell-jar full of water, which exploded as metal and liquid embraced, showering us all with silver blades, one of which punctured my neighbour's eye, distorting his vision thereafter. Our dangerous instructor, it was rumoured, lost considerably more than that: not only his job, but also his balls, sliced off by a scythe-like splinter.

To see such a grotesque dislocation between past and present in so prophetic a context brings on an attack of futurephobia, making it physically impossible for me to imagine my next move. I am as allergic to time as I am to the pollen that has infiltrated from outside. Irritating as it is, I do not mind hay fever, being such a perfectly benign example of cause and effect. In fact I quite like it, because it makes my life predictable.

"Still sneezing, Silkstone?" says the crone, signifying mutual recognition. "Oh, yes, my boy, I remember you all right. The namby-pamby Jewboy who didn't like showers with the lads. Though, I have to admit, you weren't a bad outside-right. Do you still play?"

"Just watch," I reply, "an amateur club. Wingate. But not so often as before."

"You recall the explosion?" he asks.

"Of course," I say.

"It was an accident," he says, "but afterwards I was sorry you weren't hurt. I can't explain why I took against you so. Do you think it was the instinctive dislike the Aryan feels for the Semite?"

"More likely you didn't like my face," I reply. "Others have felt the same subsequently."

"Perhaps," he says, "It is not a visage to make the spirit soar. Would you care to know if its sour expression is justified? After all, that's why you came to see me, isn't it? I bet I was quite a shock, a double-header. One, as a reminder that the past never dies; two . . . but I'm sure you've already worked that out for yourself."

"How can a man of science, a self-proclaimed worshipper of science, end up in a caravan with a monkey and a crystal ball?" I ask.

"Look into it for yourself," he replies, "then repeat your question, if you feel the need."

I see the skeleton of an umbrella. No, it is some sort of carousel, probably refracted through the bottle glass of my host's tinted window. Among the figures climbing into its carriages are my wife, our child and an elderly couple resembling my parents. As the roundabout accelerates and the spokes ascend toward the horizontal, in accordance with Newton's law, which states that freely moving bodies tend to travel in straight lines, my family begins to panic. Freely moving bodies! Ha! Einstein is right, everything is relative.

"How can I save them?" I ask.

No answer. Instead I see a rider on the wall of death, high on centrifugal force, racing to catch them when they fall.

"Is that me?" I ask.

No answer. I take fright. Newton's right, we'll rotate forever! Fortunately the clairvoyant's time is not infinite, even for me; mercenary considerations justifying Aristotle's more ancient wisdom. My family spins gently back to earth, laughing hysterically, while I spiral into an awaiting chair none the wiser.

"Well," asks my former master, "what did you see?"

England's Green and Pleasant Land

I describe it as accurately as possible.

"Actually," he says, "I'm more interested in your response. You obviously wish that the universe were really a great machine and its inhabitants all automata! Newton, as you know, believed he could predict the future of any object, given sufficient data. Using his laws it should be possible to foresee the eclipses of heavenly bodies and the fates of terrestrial ones. Would you like to know when you or those you love are going to die?"

Suddenly I feel like a prisoner in the dock watching the judge put on the black cap.

"Don't worry," he chuckles, "I haven't a clue. No life is a straight line. Not even yours. Like it or not, you are going to stray. That certainty turns everything else into probabilities. The more diversions, the longer the journey."

"That's undeniable," I say, "but how can I be sure that in prolonging my life I'm not shortening another's?"

"What do you want of me," he snaps, "gypsy charms to ward off the evil eye? Do you really think you would have saved any of them in your dream? Not a chance. No, you hung around for your own benefit, not theirs. I'm telling you to live, to take risks. Isn't that enough? If you want more you'll have to consult my marmoset."

And I have a vision of myself as an existential ape-man, the curse of "What happens next?" lifted from my shoulders by a wave of hairy irresponsibility, along with all knowledge of gravity, so that I no longer recognize the inevitability of falling, and expect each time I jump to rise higher and higher until I am flying. But there is a catch! Without "What happens next?" I have a life but no calling, lovers but no readers. Writing has turned me into my own executioner. Lunatics believe they are trapped in a plot devised elsewhere. I am more sensible. I know the trap will only spring if I act. So I don't, or haven't yet.

Exasperated, the fortune-teller grasps my wrists and holds my hands palms upwards, his thumbs pressing hard so that he can feel my racing pulse and diagnose my fear. I also look, trying to decipher the invisible book of my time to be. But all I see are sparklets of sweat, as if the Braille text were weeping.

"You are in a funk," says the clairvoyant, "scared to death of the future because it is unwritten, because it is not you who'll be writing it. You will only be happy when everything is over. Your true talent is for obituaries. On the other hand, I could be wrong. Heisenberg's uncertainty principle states that it is impossible to observe something without changing it. Look at me!"

Outside, as we stroll among the anachronisms making hay while the sun shines through the agricultural smog, my wife asks, "Well?"

"He said I'd be better off dead," I reply.

And my wife, her question answered, wonders what it will be like to be a widow.

7

Not so fast, Lena. What if there is life after death?

Allow me to introduce as evidence the gentleman presently overseeing the steam threshing-machine, certainly no ghost, though I had thought him long dead. There can be no doubt. The thick dark hair with a white streak in place of a centre parting (wider now, naturally), the snout-like nose, the flamboyant whiskers and the nose-pinching spectacles are the unmistakable characteristics of Badger, pen-name of the notorious Bruno Gascoyne, erstwhile crony of Belloc and Chesterton. Rumour had it that he killed himself (or, more kindly, that he died of a broken heart) on the night of Harold Wilson's second victory. In the missing years his shoulders have lost their military angularity and his brown tweed jacket now hangs limply, giving him the appearance of an ill-wrapped jeroboam with an anthropomorphic stopper. But his voice is as strong and his ideas as loony as ever. Love of country is still his theme, it seems, though these days its application is more practical. Hence his dramatic pose at the controls of a traction engine like some bucolic charioteer, lording it over the naked kiddies playing hide-and-seek in the chaff. Here, out of the blue, is my opportunity to overturn my father's long-forgotten defeat.

"Badger!" I shout. "Bruno Gascoyne!"

He looks at me, astonished that anyone remembers his name.

"Can we speak?" I say. "On the record."

"My dear boy," he says, quite himself again, "it will be a rare pleasure."

Nor does his *bonhomie* diminish when I reveal that I am the literary editor of the *Jewish Voice*; on the contrary, he seems delighted by the opportunity.

"I can't help feeling this is a fitting end for a writer who became a bit of a wind-bag," I say, somewhat irked by his composure.

"You don't know what you are talking about," he replies, "but you are correct. I have been betrayed like King Prasutagus, if you know who he was. Like him, or rather his widow, I am forced to witness the degradation of my daughter. If you have watched her act you have already seen more of her than any stranger should. She is a constant reminder of my failure as a father and an Englishman. Her shame is my legacy. It's not much fun being the daughter of a traitor. A traitor! A man whose creaking bones will be British till they crack. In the meantime — and you can print this — I work these old machines to maintain the pretence that there is still a benign relationship between human evolution and the exploitation of the land. Though we all know that fertilizer, not magic, ensures the seasonal harvest. No, the land has lost its gods. Just as our country has mislaid its story. Deprived of a sustaining epic a nation will quickly lose its identity. Or, in the more eloquent words of my friend Tom Eliot: 'A people without history is not redeemed from time.' That is why your people have survived so long, why Jerusalem is once again your capital. Because you have never forgotten. It amuses me to watch the Palestinians, for whom I have much sympathy, trying to mould their own national myth out of your words. But then I am easily amused nowadays, being somewhat removed from the fray. So let's be banal. Football, like our nation, is in decline because teams have sold their collective spirit for the sake of a few players' *amour propre*. Manchester United had a story, so did Spurs, long before the Tottenham Yids. Not any more."

Nor Wingate, I think, not since they accepted Gentile players. To sacrifice identity in pursuit of victory, I realize, removes the possibility of tragedy, an essential element in any story.

"You speak warmly of Israel." I say, "That is a surprise from such a well-known anti-Semite."

"It is very foolish to equate anti-Zionism and anti-Semitism," he replies. "In my experience many anti-Zionists have your best interests at heart. They want to think well of Jews. Only real anti-Semites are Zionists. They have no interest how Jews behave in their own country so long as they stay there. Indeed, if Israel were the only Jewish state I would have no quarrel with Jews at all. But, like Joseph, you won't stay at home, nor will you rest until you control the countries you colonize. You are political chameleons, each with your coat of many colours. Red for Russia, blue for Britain, something a little jazzier for the United States."

"Some years ago I heard you blame the last two wars upon the Jews," I say. "My father, also present, called you a liar. You declined to answer. Are you prepared to do so now?"

"By all means, my dear boy!" he replies. "It will be my pleasure to enlighten readers of the *Jewish Voice*. The First World War was probably an accident, an unforeseen side-effect of the Dreyfus case, which destroyed the French Intelligence Bureau and so allowed the Germans to surprise the garrisons at Mons and Charleroi. No doubt many genuinely believed Dreyfus to have been wrongly convicted, but just as many were out to restore the immunity usually bestowed upon those members of that very powerful clique of international financiers to which

Dreyfus was affiliated. Well, they won and destroyed Europe in the process, though not before they had made a tidy profit by selling arms to both sides. I must confess that when I spoke about the Second War on the occasion you referred to, I was relying upon intuition, but now, I am glad to inform your readers, thanks to papers obtained by scholars from the Institute for Historical Research under the Freedom of Information Act, I have proof positive. It seems that in a series of secret meetings at Casablanca and Rabat a group representing America's richest barons negotiated a deal with the then Arab potentates whereby they would remove the threat of European Jewry, which at last seemed interested in reclaiming its Middle Eastern birthright, in exchange for cheap oil. As a result a certain Corporal Schicklgrüber suddenly found himself with inexhaustible funds. The Americans were all circumcised according to their custom, as were the bankers who financed Hitler. Of course, after the war, they double-crossed their one-time allies and forced the State of Israel upon them. But that, as we know, is another story."

"Do you have any plans for the future?" I ask.

"To die," he replies, "to give you the pleasure of composing my obituary."

That night, when I am reading to Joshua, he asks, "Was that old man your grandfather?"

"No," I say, "I haven't got a grandfather any more."

"Why?" asks Joshua. "Did someone kill him?"

"No," I say.

"Did he die?" he asks.

"Yes," I say.

"Why?" he asks.

"He was old," I say, "he got worn out."

"Will my mummy die?" he asks. I hesitate. "Will you die?" he continues.

"Probably," I say.

"Will I die?" he asks.

"I hope not," I say. *Fuck you, death,* I think. *Leave my little boy alone.*

95

8

The following day Bruno Gascoyne's real daughter echoes my demand, "Leave my father alone." Except, of course, she is addressing me. The anger in her eyes, already well established, is now for my benefit alone. Her hatred, a palpable presence, crashes around my office like a demented gargoyle.

I should have anticipated this call, of course. But I could hardly have predicted her companion. Having long since returned his librarian to her shelves, Adam Smith has at last let his hair down and plucked the rose of Sharon, a lily among the thorny daughters of Albion, an apple tree among the trees of the wood, whose fruit is sweet to his taste.

In his last month at Kingsland Meadow a group of hippies had set up camp in the shade of the spoil heap. At night, around a fire they recited poems (identified as William Blake's by the librarian, who recognized "The Sick Rose"), roasted potatoes, and smoked marijuana, the aroma of which excited Adam's imagination, its legend being as potent as its hallucinogenic properties.

He took to strolling across the excavation at dawn so that he could watch Sharon emerge, as naked as Venus, from her crimson sleeping-bag. She squatted behind a bush, unconcerned that her animal activities were being observed, and sat down for breakfast wearing nothing but an oriental wrap. One morning he caught her staring at the mosaic, as if at her own reflection in a pool, and in a vision he saw the house entire as it was then, fifteen hundred years earlier. Had he brought the past to life, or was he merely a filament from the future, an invisible time-traveller? Either way, she became, in that instant, a part of the dig, a living artefact, as much a feature of Kingsland Meadow as the villa's foundations or the mysterious skeleton. But, unlike that unfortunate, she had flesh on the bone, as he was destined to know.

England's Green and Pleasant Land

They were lovers until she vanished that spring of '82, only returning a fortnight ago, by which time Adam Smith could quote the poetry of William Blake by heart, so that when he saw, through the early morning mist, that the meadow had been transformed into a caravanserai he thought of "the Sons & Daughters of Albion on soft clouds, waking from sleep".

Sharon introduced Adam to her father, hence his appearance as character witness for the defence.

"Why has the *Jewish Voice* got it in for Badger?" he says. "How can he be an anti-Semite when he believes that the Lost Tribes of Israel washed up on Albion's shores?"

"Adam," I say, "have you gone soft in the head? Or have you fallen for his *constructive* sentimentality? Do you fancy yourself as his little Albert Speer?"

"What's so wrong with wanting to build a new Jerusalem?" he demands. "Maybe we should appeal to your readers."

"Listen," says Sharon, "my father is nearly ninety. He's a forgotten man. I'd like to keep it that way. Publish your interview and the attention will destroy him. Is that what you want? Do you hate him that much? I beg of you, Mr Silkstone, leave my father alone."

"Why this sudden concern?" I say. "Do you think displaying your fanny in public is good for his health?"

At which the gargoyle strikes: something or someone tries to tear out my eyes.

"That was below the belt," says Adam, rescuing me none the less.

"What else do you expect from a fucking Yid?" cries Albion's daughter. As an afterthought she adds, "May you rot in hell," as if she had some influence in the matter.

Her last remarks nearly persuade me, but then I recall how Bruno Gascoyne humiliated my father in public, so, as soon as they are gone, I send the interview to the printers. The gargoyle, now perched on a cornice, shakes its head, more in sorrow than in anger.

9

Two weeks later I publish it in the *Jewish Voice* under the title: "Father of Albion". The following day Old Maxie the office postman calls me down to his cubby-hole.

"It's addressed to you," he says, pointing out a rank-smelling manila envelope.

"It doesn't contain vanilla ice cream, that's for sure," I say. "Throw it away."

"There are some letters as well," says Old Maxie.

My correspondents all hate me. Some because I have lampooned their hero, others because I have revived their arch-enemy. "I fail to understand," writes one of the latter, "that you needed two columns of space in the *Jewish Voice* to interview B. Gascoyne to say nothing pertaining to anything about his life of Jew-hating. In these days of renewed activity of Jew-haters you should devote valuable space to write a lot of *bullshit* and nothing of interest of his anti-Semitic activities suggests that as a reviewer in a Hebrew journal you would be better employed as a pen-pusher for the British Party. It seems to me that you are a renegade Jew who changed his name or a Jew-hating bastard. The present editor is obviously not very particular in what his contributors' views are. Even so I am surprised you can get payment for your dirty rotten bullshit. To hell with you, you dirty renegade." The final envelope contains a death threat. I'm still deciding what to do about it when the phone rings.

"They tell me you are a friend of Jerry Unger," begins my caller.

"Hardly," I say. "I'm talking to him next week about his new novel. That's the extent of our friendship."

"So," he replies, "give me his address anyway. Why? Because I have something he needs. It is the truth. About the Jews. He is a genius, they will listen to him. Me? I am nothing. Next week I have to go into hospital. Too much sugar in my blood. Or not enough. What difference? I am finished anyway. My kidneys, liver, heart, spleen; all gone

98

to pot. That I am alive so long is a miracle. Forty camps I survived. The Nazis couldn't kill me. It took your friends to finish me off. Jews? Them? No, they are English gentlemen. And you are as bad as the rest of them. Why won't you give me his address? You think I want to sleep with him? Listen, for the sake of your conscience, I'll make an exception. Jerry Unger I won't fuck. It's a promise. Now will you give me his address?

"Testimony I have given to both Houses of Parliament. You can look me up in Hansard. Dates I'll give you later. But Jerry Unger I'm not allowed to talk to. Why do I want him? Because he's not afraid of the truth. Which is: we weren't all saints, nor were the Nazis all monsters. That other writer, what's his name? The one who wrote *The Odessa File*. That's right, Frederick Forsyth. He called Edvard Roschmann the Butcher of Riga. It is a slander. Who knows better than me? I worked in his office. He was no saint. How could he be in such a position? But he was no murderer either. Forsyth doesn't know what he's talking about. Once he caught a Jew bare-bottom with a German nurse. He could have killed him. Bang. Bang. No problem. Intercourse with Aryans being a capital crime. Instead he said, 'Let the Jew live.' Later, by a miracle, the same Jew turned up in a selection. Again he let him live. This man Forsyth calls the Butcher of Riga.

"Even in winter the Germans didn't starve. They had enough left over to feed the birds. Sparrows could eat. But God help a Jew who picked up a crust. Better hunger than death. Well, this so-called butcher collected the scraps from the snow and delivered them personally to the Jewish hospital. No one wants to hear such things. You don't want to know either. I've had enough. I survived forty camps, so one address I'll find for myself.

"Who is Jerry Unger anyway? A member of the Royal Family? The Queen of England? Much she knows. In fact, I know more about what's going on in her country than she does. They are everywhere. And you know who I mean by *they*. Only the other day the Queen Mother took the salute at a parade of SS troopers. Where? Near Coventry. It was in the local papers. How do I know? Believe me. At Riga I worked in the office of five Gestapo generals. I have recognized one. Here in England. Now he is very respectable. A public figure. Another Nazi is a Member of Parliament. I have seen him with my own eyes. He has changed his name, of course. But not his views. One day I shall expose him. Not today. It's not safe that you should know who he is. You see how I look after you? Jerry Unger has nothing to fear from me.

"It's happening again. What I saw in Germany. But who will listen to me? I am not Jerry Unger. Nor even, excuse me, Jake Silkstone. My friend, already you have listened to me longer than anyone else. For that I congratulate you. Your colleagues put down the receiver as soon as they hear my name. The *Voice* yes, *Pravda* no. They don't want to hear the truth.

"But I am telling you that, even as we speak, Nazis are training new recruits all over the country. I am not talking about skinheads or glue-sniffers or punks or the British Party. No, Jake, I am thinking of English gentlemen. The sort your Jewish compatriots admire so much. If you don't believe me, ask your new friend Bruno Gascoyne. I read your interview with him. You are a very clever young man, but I don't think you have any idea how dangerous he is. I used to know him, before the war. He was as *meshugge* in his way as my other friend, Orde Wingate. Both were obsessed with Jews; Bruno hated them, Orde couldn't have too much of us. One taught us how to kill, now the other is persuading our enemies to finish us off.

"I would like to say: let us meet, here are my proofs. But next week I am going into hospital. If I come out again I'll be surprised. You name it, I've got it. Angina, cancer, diabetes. The Nazis started the job, now your lot are finishing it.

"You have been very patient, my friend. I hope I will have the opportunity to talk with you again. But I have the feeling that my luck has run out. Perhaps you think I am

100

wrong to complain. I should be grateful that I survived the war. I should say thanks to God for making me one of the living dead. But when my chance came to have some sort of life big-shot Jews in Hollywood pulled the rug away. I starred in a movie with Marlon Brando. But did anyone see it? No. Because *they* decided not to distribute it. Listen, you are a writer, I have a story. We need one another. You can be my ghost-writer, the ghost of a ghost. In the meantime I'll send you a letter. Read it. Then, if in your wisdom you decide I'm not crazy, pass it on to Unger."

10

"What shall I do about it?" I ask my wife.

"About what?" she says.

"The death threat," I reply.

"We're all going to die," she says.

"This isn't psychosomatic," I say, "I've got it in writing."

"Did you show it to the editor?" she asks.

I nod.

"What did he think?" she asks.

"He said the fellow had a point," I say. Lena smiles. "You don't seem much more sympathetic," I say.

"Look at the handwriting," she says, "the man's a nutcase. He can't even hold the pen steady enough to cross a 't', so I doubt he'll be able to cut your throat."

This graphological insight would be a clincher if it weren't for Uzi's assassination, not to mention the bomb that blew off the hands of our cleaning woman. Just as I am supposed to have forgotten about my wife's infidelities with the late, lamented cultural attaché and the still vital Polish poet, it seems I am also expected to have erased the former's unpleasant end from my memory, not to mention my own scriptophobia.

At the same time, it must be said, the man who threatened to chop one of the *Voice's* reporters into potato chips turned out, upon investigation, to be a respectable gent, a buyer for one of the great department stores, whose violent instincts had hitherto been directed in time-honoured fashion against the animals of the field. At his trial he pleaded guilty, his lawyer claiming in mitigation that he had been very upset by the nightly newsreels from the Lebanon. The judge, passing sentence, said that even so he shouldn't make threats against decent Jews. He was given a suspended sentence. His employers, the afore-mentioned store, decided to keep him on. Not every pain is a cancer, I conclude, nor every crank a murderer. Forget about them and they'll probably vanish.

Instead I worry, as usual, about the silent killers who send no advance warnings, in the hope of pre-empting their surprise attack. It works! I survive the following week. Long enough to see the famous American émigré, Jerry Unger, matchmaker and novelist, to whom I go without the packet promised by my other correspondent.

As an adolescent I thrived on the disreputable antics of his heroes, amazed and delighted that the vernacular of my subconscious could become — of all things! — literature. Needless to say, the elders of Zion weren't quite so thrilled, and the message was drummed from *bima* to *bima* that Unger was a betrayer of his people. Angered despite him-self, he concocted a series of fierce self-obsessed fictions charting the development of the writer Unger would have been if he were the person his enemies said he was.

As it turns out, he isn't the person I thought he was either; in other words, he isn't me. Expensively dressed, he looks every inch the Anglophile, completely at home in the smart hotel, ties obligatory, to which he has invited me. He speaks about his books with a detachment not evident in his prose.

"To what am I a traitor?" he asks. "Judaism? OK, I plead guilty to eating pork. Is that so terrible?"

"It was when I was a kid," I say. "I remember Rabbi Nathan, our local saint, denouncing a butcher who painted a Mogen David on his window, through which could be seen joints of pork."

"Eating is one thing," says Unger, "selling another. I don't pretend to be kosher. Pushing pork on the unsuspecting isn't my line."

"In that case," I say, "you're a better man than me."

"I doubt it," says Unger. "No, the reason they hate me is because I don't peddle nostalgia, because I don't, unlike your Bruno Gascoynes, base all my social intercourse upon an imaginary past. Don't get me wrong, I'm all for rebuilding Jerusalem. Just let a Gentile put down Israel in my presence! But I defend it because it's there. Not on account of some sentimental attachment to the Bible. Frankly, the much loved Jewish tradition means zilch to me. Why not ask BG (and I don't mean Ben-Gurion) these questions? After all, he betrayed his country. All I've betrayed is the big secret that a Jew without his clothes acts like anyone else. I try to tell the truth as I see it. Is that such a crime? Does it really put me in the same league as Goebbels and Streicher?"

"That reminds me," I say, "I had a lunatic on the phone the other day asking for you. At least I thought he was a lunatic. But it turned out that his craziest claim — that he starred in a movie with Marlon Brando — was true. The rest doesn't seem so crazy any more."

"What did he want?" asks Unger.

"Well," I say, "he didn't want to fuck you."

"That's a good start," says Unger.

"He thinks you're not afraid of the truth," I say.

"Which is?" says Unger.

"That not all Jews are saints," I say.

"Is that all?" says Unger.

"He wanted to tell you the story of his life and terrible times," I say, "of his escapades in forty death camps, of his belief that history is repeating itself in this green and pleasant land."

"So next time give him my address," says the scribe. "I'm always interested in a good yarn."

"Mr Unger," I reply, "don't you ever feel like a grave-robber?"

Blood Libels

"Some people are up to their knees in gore," says Unger. "We're up to our knees in history, which happens to be full of dead Jews. You're right, I'm a vampire, I suck stories from corpses. How else can a Jewish writer join the immortals?"

"So you are a Jewish writer?" I say.

"A sacrilegious one," he says.

"Did you never feel a conflict between your religion and your talent," I ask, "given the direction of the latter?"

"The guilt I write about is not mine," he says. "My father is proud of me. He would forgive me anything."

"Even patricide?" I ask. "In *The Revenge of Isaac* didn't you confess that your naïve Oedipal desire to bump off your old man was hopelessly compromised by the fact that the Germans were thinking along the same lines? Lines that led to Auschwitz. Didn't the ghost of your father accuse you of having a Nazi imagination? Isn't that why you gave him the last word? To prove that you haven't?"

"Listen," says Unger, "you're confusing me with my character. Izzy Smolinsky feels guilty. Not me. Let's leave it at that. To tell you the truth, I'm sick of Smolinsky. I don't want to write about him any more. The trouble is that I don't seem able to write about anyone else. What do you think of Smolinsky? Shall I stick with him?"

Having seen something of myself in Smolinsky I naturally feel inclined to defend him.

"Why do you ask?" I enquire.

"Because I'm thinking of killing him off," replies Unger. "In fact, just between the two of us, that's what I'm doing right how. And it's fun. It's like attending your own funeral. You even get to write your own obits."

"One of my duties at the *Voice* is compiling literary obituaries," I say. "If you spare Smolinsky I'll let you write yours for real."

"Ah," says Unger, "a bribe from the Angel of Death."

104

The Angel of Death? Me? The man who rides the wall of death hoping to save others from falling into the pit. Meanwhile, up above, the genuine Angel of Death burnishes his wings, for it is the eve of Rosh Hashana when God dips his quill in blood and decides whose name to inscribe in the Book of Life and whose to pass on to his hired killer. With each name the bones in his arms, from the shoulder-blade to the smallest phalange, glow redder and redder until his hands ignite and the hot air sends him spiralling on his perennial mission.

As I drive home I recall the song my father used to sing on Seder Night, *"Had Gadya, Had Gadya"*: only one kid. A cat eats the kid, a dog bites the cat, a stick beats the dog, a fire burns the stick, water quenches the fire, an ox drinks the water, a slaughterer butchers the ox, and the Angel of Death slays the butcher. However, his triumph is short-lived, at least in the song, for along comes the Holy One, blessed be He, who destroys the Angel of Death.

But not this year, I fear, not with the Israelis on the outskirts of Beirut.

No doubt in Tel Aviv, at this very moment, Hannah Ben-Tur is lighting the shabbat candles, wishing she knew the whereabouts of her husband, somewhere north of the border. It's more than I deserve, but last week she sat down at her kitchen table when the kids were all asleep and wrote the following sentence: "To tell you the truth, it began as a game, I never really expected you to take it seriously, but when you did and we kissed and I felt you climbing up my belly, I suddenly realized that I really, really wanted you to fuck me, but you didn't, you fool — come to my house and I'll give you one more chance."

The rest of the letter is less libidinous; on the contrary, it is a quotation from her husband's last to her. "Just so you know of one Israeli soldier up there," she wrote, "who isn't part of an efficient fighting machine, as our army is called by outsiders these days."

Blood Libels

It is a warm night, practically the last of the summer, made monochrome by the transparent darkness. Decisions are easy, everything being black and white, but as usual I make the wrong one. I decide without a qualm to take a diversion and invite Hannah Ben-Tur on an imaginary date to Kingsland Meadow.

As I turn off the main road I notice in my mirror a pair of cock-eyed headlights trailing me. Next time I look they are gone, which is odd, because the road leads nowhere else.

Succumbing to a nocturne on the radio I pull off beside the white gate, where it is possible to read the letter by moonlight. But it is Hannah's husband, Ami Ben-Tur, who dominates the proceedings. We may be on the brink of infidelity, but he is looking into the void.

"It's just like on the telly — everyone sitting on the guns and zeldas, the girls and boys singing the old favourites, the hills all around," he wrote. "Maybe we'll be in Beirut in three hours, maybe tomorrow, maybe never. If we do go in, it will be horrible. Today we were practising urban house-to-house fighting. Watching these guys (my age, two to three kids) doing the whole thing — grenade through the door, burst in shooting, next pair up the stairs — made me so sad. Only funny thing was being instructed to blow up the Hilton. Hope we'll be able to have a good laugh over it in the one back home. The guys in the tent are discussing the number of expected dead if we go in. Estimates range from 300 to over 1,000. I think I'm glad we won't be fighting from the zeldas. It's claustrophobic inside, as well as being a big target with a ton of explosive on board. I'm not so scared as sad for you and everyone if anything happens to me. Not that I think I'm any great loss. It's just so tragic. I'm worried that when it all starts I won't function properly or I won't rescue somebody whom I should or I'll try to help someone I shouldn't or I'll help civilians and neglect our lot or the opposite or I'll have the shits or shoot one of our lot or drop a hand grenade or any of the thousand things I might do wrong. As if that wasn't enough, I've got about three times the stuff I'd normally carry, plus belt with ten magazines, flak jacket, helmet, goggles, gun, stretcher. It is now twenty-four hours since we were told we were going in. Twelve hours ago we were packed up, in formation, with the engines running, when it was postponed. God knows what the long-term effects of all this are going to be on our mental health. It's getting dark, so I'll have to stop. The batteries in my torch are running low. Besides, there's a story going the rounds that the medics have taken on two girls from Tzur, given them a monthly salary of 150,000 shekels, and installed them in the hospital tent."

I reconsider the last lines. Am I meant to read between them? They certainly balance Hannah's invitation. Perhaps she wants me to know that her husband is a bit of a devil and doesn't expect his wife to be any better. *So go to the tents of Tzur, I think, and find your pleasure there, while your wife whispers in my ear, "I really, really want you to fuck me."*

Her hands seek out my obedient member and, having exposed it to nocturnal predators, begin to give it further encouragement, bringing forth a droplet of quicksilver, eternal messenger between the generations. Delivery is just about to be completed when I hear a low growl outside the car, following by a flapping of wings as something uncanny lands on the roof. In my frenzy I assume that the Angel of Death is on the last chore of the old year. Just my luck, I think, to meet my Maker *in flagrante delicto.*

But the pock-marked, tattooed, bearded and scarred face that is suspended the wrong way up on the night side of my windscreen is too grotesque to sustain that delusion. The glass fractures, not because of supernatural ugliness without, but because a hammer has shattered it. Then a hand crashes through, its wrist protected by a studded gauntlet, that grabs the tie I had specially put on for the meeting with Unger, hardly a capital offence.

Normally, I suppose, a man being choked will try to loosen the noose, but I am equally concerned with protecting my private parts from flying glass, a consideration that probably saves my life. For my hands are free, beyond the hangman's reach, allowing me to start the motor and drive straight at the gate, thereby somersaulting my assailant into the meadow. Whereupon his accomplice emerges from the shadows.

Driving is no easy matter with pants around your ankles, believe me, but there is little time for niceties when you are in flight from a solitary Hell's Angel intent upon redeeming his clip-winged companion's fall. Cursing Karl Werner's uncertainty principle, I reach the main road and, thank God, the bosom of my family.

"What were you doing at Kingsland Meadow?" asks Lena.

"I wanted to think over the interview with Unger," I say, "to play back the tape in peace and quiet."

"Did you have it on loud?" she asks.

"No," I say. "What difference?"

"Maybe you disturbed someone," she says.

"Enough for them to try to strangle me?" I say.

"Why else would they attack you?" she asks.

I can think of two reasons: retribution for my attempted adultery with a succuba, revenge for my interview — with Gascoyne, not Unger.

"I did get a death threat," I remind my wife.

"You'd better call the police," she replies.

Joshua, awakened by my dramatic entry, wants to know every detail, much to Lena's despair. "Was it a monster," he asks, "or a robber?"

"A monstrous robber," I reply.

"Did he cut off your head?" he asks.

"He wanted to," I reply.

"Did you chop him to pieces?" he asks.

"Yes," I reply, "but then he got up and chased me home."

"Is he outside now?" asks my son.

"No," I reply, "he's right here." I hunch my shoulders. I waggle my hands. I growl. I'm a monster!

Joshua, terrified, runs to his mother, taken in by the

metamorphosis. And why not? Observation suggests his Daddy is immutable, but this doesn't preclude the possiblity of his sudden transfiguration. All his books tell him it can happen, not to mention quantum mechanics, which proclaims that our reality is subjective.

"Daddy's just pretending," says Lena, no less gullible than he, having already swallowed my lie.

12

As befits a man who has outfaced death, I feel inclined to make love and I find Lena in a reciprocal mood. But I am like a man cursed with priapism; no amount of connubial passion can deflate my tumid desire. Nor can I sleep. Once, at a publisher's party, I met a beautiful woman who described how she went astral-tripping when captivated by insomnia. It seems that her ectoplasmic self would rise from her corporeal entity and float whither she fancied. Thus she was able to discover who was sleeping with whom, though she wouldn't sell her secrets for all the tea in China.

I consider astral-tripping to Tel Aviv but finally settle upon the World Service of the BBC, which promptly transports me to the very spot. However, it isn't words of love that I hear. By the morning I have recomposed the front page of the *Jewish Voice*. No longer does the headline say: "LIT ED WRESTLES WITH ANGEL." Instead it must deal with an event that began in another part of the world, the important bit, about the same time as I was fighting for my life. By comparison that incident now seems comic.

The story, written by the editor, which appears the following Friday begins thus:

In one of the most traumatic weeks in Israel's history the nation has been rent by bitter argument as to whether the country's leadership bears a responsibility in the massacre of Palestinians by Christian Phalange forces in two Beirut refugee camps on September 16 and 17.

At the subsequent editorial meeting he expresses regret for having allowed me to publish anything about Bruno Gascoyne.

"The last thing we need at a time like this," he says, "is for our enemies to have an acceptable figurehead. Mark my words, this massacre — if that's what it is — will make anti-Semitism fashionable again. And we've given them a hero!"

Sure enough, *The Times* invites Gascoyne to contribute a feature in which he assures the Christian world that it need no longer feel guilt on account of the holocaust, since the Jews have proved themselves equally adept at genocide. "The worm has turned," he concludes, "and it is time for the blackbird to sing."

Naturally enough this provokes a bitter exchange, not least in the *Jewish Voice*, making nonsense of Gascoyne's assertion of Jewish silence in the wake of such an outrage. The Chief Rabbi, writing to *The Times*, feels compelled to allude to "the fierce moral debates convulsing Jewish communities everywhere, including Anglo-Jewry", as well as to the 400,000 Israelis who demonstrated against the Likud administration ("corresponding to 6 million British citizens turning up to protest against their government in wartime" — how the Chief Rabbi must have enjoyed writing that figure!).

My hives reappear with a vengeance, as if I were blaming myself for the forthcoming pogrom. The doctor gives me some ointment.

"Whatever you do, don't scratch," he says, advice on everyone's lips.

Maybe I'm over-valuing my symptoms, maybe my body is merely anticipating the savage embraces of Hannah Ben-Tur.

Her latest letter is another duet, likewise mixing love and war. "They say stress causes cancer," she wrote, "so you'd better get here quick. Otherwise you're likely to find a half-bald, breastless skeleton. Will you still want me then? Don't worry, you'll be spared that dilemma, because pretty soon there won't be a *here* to get to. The country is going down the tubes, and it's dragging us all with it. Ami returned from the Lebanon heartbroken. He couldn't believe what our army was doing, but even worse was what the PLO had already done. Near his camp was an old woman with her five or six daughters. She kept bringing them food. Tears were always in her eyes. She said that the PLO had taken away her husband and sons and killed them. To her Ami was a liberator. He didn't feel like one. He is convinced that our only hope is to disengage ourselves from the West Bank, but he knows equally well that once we are gone the whole area will become a bloodbath as the various factions of the PLO fight for their pound of flesh, and it won't be long before the poor felleen are fondly remembering the good old days of the Israeli occupation, which we'll probably have to re-establish. But the first thing is to get us out of the Lebanon.

"Ami goes to all the demonstrations. He came back from the Lebanon angry, but strong, from these he comes home shaking like an old man. It isn't Arabs screaming 'Kibbutznikim sons of bitches' and 'Fascistim' at him but other Jews! It isn't Arabs spitting at him but his own people! It isn't Arabs pelting him with empty Coke cans but fellow Israelis. He is convinced that one day a maniac will throw a grenade. And it won't be an Arab! Oh, please, Jake, come and fuck me so that I can forget everything! Come, before it's too late!"

But, unknown to me, different travel arrangements have been made on my behalf by the omniscient author of all our stories.

13

As if to endorse the Chief Rabbi's claim that fierce moral debates are convulsing Anglo-Jewry, Asa Dorfman the doorman and Old Maxie the office postman come to blows over the business at Sabra and Shatilla.

"Goys kill goys," shouts the former, "and they hang the Jews."

"Hypocrite!" screeches the latter. "The Israelis are no different from the Tsarist police who let the Cossacks into the *shtetlach* and then claimed their hands were clean."

This is too much for our excitable Chief of Security. He begins to slap his tormentor, who laughs with triumph, having at last provoked the reactionary backlash that, according to all revolutionary theory, will inevitably bring about a new dawn. Several members of staff, including Meir the Printer, try to pull the adversaries apart, but with no success.

Thus it is that three personable young men are able to breach our normally tight security, by claiming an appointment with the editor and gaining admittance from a distracted secretary who is more concerned about explaining the fracas to the visitors than checking their identities.

"Tempers are a little short at present," she mutters as she escorts them to the lift.

By the time the doors open on to the second floor they have removed the automatic pistols from their hiding places. They grab the nearest secretary, conveniently placed, being late for her appointment at the ante-natal clinic, and too far gone to use the stairs.

"OK, you Jewish cunt," hisses A, "where's the editor?"

She doesn't say, probably because she is outraged by his language.

"Is he worth dying for?" asks B.

"He's not here," she whispers. "He's gone to a press briefing at the Embassy with the news editor."

"So who's around?" asks C.

"Only the travel editor," she replies, "and the literary editor."

"He'll have to do," says A. "Where's his office?"

She points to my door.

There's quite a crowd around the fire-escape to watch

me go, among them the secretary who gave me away. I try to cheer her up.

"Some writers will do anything to get a review," I say.

"They think this is a joke," says A. "I'll soon wipe the smiles off their Jew faces. This is for you, cunt, to stop you bringing any more Yid bastards into the world." Calmly taking aim, he shoots the unfortunate secretary in her right breast, which begins to lactate blood as if he were performing a miracle rather than a murder.

She looks at her hand in disbelief, then begins to sway, thus presenting a harder target, which does not prevent the gunman from placing a second bullet between her eyes. These convey her last thoughts to us all: "Help me, please, don't let me die."

Bruno Gascoyne is furious. "I must apologize for the behaviour of this scum," he says. "The sad fact is that your typical anti-Semite is no longer a gentleman. I have endeavoured to halt this decline but, as you witnessed this afternoon, I am engaged in an uphill battle. Sharon — that's my daughter, you'll recall — explained the layout of your department to these animals, she even drew them a map, so they knew exactly where the editor was. All they had to do was collect him. Needless to say, they had strict instructions not to harm a soul in the process. So what do they do? They murder a pregnant woman — please accept my condolences for the death of that poor girl — and kidnap the wrong man.

"My dear sir, your company is a delight, but I'm afraid that you are of no use to me at all. The idea was to reach a private arrangement whereby the *Jewish Voice* would publish a statement concocted by myself and a few colleagues in exchange for your editor's life. Now, with a body on the premises, the police are bound to be called, and the whole affair will become public somewhat prematurely. Nor, my dear fellow, despite the esteem in which we all hold you, do I think you possess much value in the bazaar. In short, Mr Silkstone, you are something of a white elephant. But how can I let you go? In the words of

Mr Hitchcock, you are a man who knows too much." He shrugs. "Can you give me one good reason why I shouldn't order my trigger-happy yeomen to shoot you like a dog?"

Concentrate! What was the basis of my appeal to Unger when I tried to persuade him to commute Smolinsky's death sentence?

"If you bump him off," I had said, "the energy of those early books will be wasted. No longer will it be possible to laugh spontaneously at the comic bits. We all know he won't live to be a hundred and twenty but an unwritten death creates the illusion of immortality. Grant him that. He's too nice to die and you're too kind to kill him."

"That's what you think," Unger had replied.

My eloquence was found wanting then, and is unlikely to be any more appreciated now. Who has a harder heart than a writer? Only a politician!

I remember Ami's words, written on the eve of battle. How right he was! I am not scared, nor even depressed. Melancholy is the *mot juste*. I wonder what Lena will tell Joshua, and imagine him calling for me in the hope of yet another magic transformation. At which I nearly crack. But I am too angry to beg for mercy. Fuck Gascoyne. Fuck my fate. What will my friends say about me at the funeral? Who, if any, will cry? What will become of my books? Will Lena keep them all? How soon will she take a new lover? It won't be long, if her behaviour when I was alive is any guide. This is amusing. I recognize the perverse pleasure Unger must have felt in doing away with Smolinsky. Except, of course, that I am flesh and blood.

Like Ami, I begin to worry that I won't acquit myself well when my time comes. *Please*, I pray, *don't let me shit in my pants*. If Lena wants to put her finger up my anus when we fuck that's OK but, inconsistent or not, I insist upon shitting in private. If I don't let my wife watch me, I'd rather not let my executioner in on the act.

"Cat got your tongue?" says Bruno Gascoyne. "Well, you can relax. I've decided to spare you, at least for tonight, unless you really have lost your voice. These days I don't

England's Green and Pleasant Land

often have the opportunity of crossing swords with a genuine Jewish intellectual. That's why killing you before dinner would be a criminal waste. The morons here, among whom I am condemned to live out my life, know bugger all about literature. Most of them don't even know why they're called The Children of Albion."

Armed pickets now man the perimeter of Kingsland Meadow whistling, of all things, tunes of the Confederate South. From the centre of the field where I am sitting cross-legged at Gascoyne's right hand, they look like supernatural creatures of the night kept at bay by the camp-fire which is, simultaneously, charring our beef steaks. Our appetites aroused by the insidious aroma of burning flesh *al fresco*, we pass a stoneware flagon from hand to hand, taking heady gulps of honey-scented mead; from Gascoyne to me, to Sharon, from her to Adam Smith, and from him to two members of the Popular Front for the Liberation of Palestine, who toast the guns that will clear the road to peace and liberation.

"I suppose you're surprised to see me breaking bread with such off-white fellows," says Gascoyne. "Marxist-Leninists to boot. But, as the proverb goes, my enemy's enemy is my friend. Our common foe being, naturally, the international Zionist conspiracy. It got us into two wars and now, if we do nothing, it's going to get us into a third, which will be the end of us all. As a consequence I must now contradict one of my earlier remarks. It does seem to matter how you behave in your own country, or rather in the land you stole from these chaps. They don't want you there, we don't want you here. So where's left for the wandering Jew? I don't want to hurt your feelings, but the inescapable conclusion is that Hitler knew what he was about all the time. The man was a prophet!"

Dying flames reflected from the fire dance in his eyes, creating the illusion that primitive pyres are burning within his skull. Later the glow from the embers turns his eyes red, like those of a nocturnal predator caught at the kill by a better hunter's flashlight. Not only is Gascoyne the

115

slaughterer, I realize, he is also the altar. He has been touched by divine madness; he believes in his own divinity!

"I will sing you a song of Los, the Eternal Prophet:
He sung it to four harps at the tables of Eternity."

His voice is tuneless but powerful, turning the poem into a primitive chant that heats the blood of his companions, though none could say why, for not a syllable do they understand. Gascoyne pauses. He listens carefully, as if expecting a message, and sure enough the sibylline darkness offers the hooting of owls.

"They have reason to be grateful," he says. "The birds we trapped will fill their bellies until winter." Then he looks at me and resumes his chant, very slowly, making sure that I don't miss a word.

"Thus the terrible race of Los & Enitharmon gave
Laws & Religions to the sons of Har, binding them
   more
And more to Earth, closing and restraining,
Till a Philosophy of Five Senses was complete.
Urizen wept & gave it into the hands of Newton &
   Locke."

He stops again and I realize that we are at the heart of an improvised ritual which, I fear, may demand a rather more substantial sacrifice than the hermaphrodite ox we have yet to taste. There is, in fact, a general uneasiness, as though all feared Gascoyne was about to demand an interpretation of them. Only the owls, who encircle us, dare to express their opinion freely.

"Mr Silkstone," he says at last, "I should like to give you a demonstration of what good progress my charges are making." Cupping his hands over his mouth he shouts, "Children, the terrible race of Los. Who are they?"

And out of the darkness, again and again, comes the answer, "The Jews!"

"Were Blake alive today," continues Gascoyne, "he would undoubtedly add Einstein to the list. After all, he's the greatest criminal of the twentieth century, father of the atom bomb, with which the Yids intend to hold the world to ransom, until Rothschild's coffers overflow with the Vatican's gold. Oh, but I will do more than preserve the Pontiff's trinkets! I intend to unseat Urizen, your Yahveh, in the name of humanity. Our spirits are infinite, but they are enslaved by His iron-clad laws. Mr Silkstone, you are my witness, I challenge God to mortal combat! Bring me my Bow of burning gold! Bring me my Chariot of fire!"

I cannot believe that these are anything more than rhetorical flourishes, that Gascoyne really anticipates such a titanic struggle, but God pulls a fast one and that's what he gets. Before our eyes the owls emerge from the peripheral darkness materialized as men who, nevertheless, are able to scatter the guards as if the latter were mice. "The Jews, the Jews!" once more echoes around the meadow, but the warning comes too late, and our circle is surrounded by the word made flesh. Armed with Uzis they stand as still as peristaliths guarding the unburied dead.

Gascoyne's mouth is open, but his overwhelming defeat has rendered him speechless. Sharon smoulders hotter than the coal, radiating hatred on her father's behalf. Adam looks awe-struck, convinced that a crack unit of the Israeli army has turned up to rescue me. The stubble-chinned Palestinian to his right jumps to his feet, as if courting a martyr's death, and is unceremoniously knocked senseless by a single blow from a gun-butt. Thereafter no one dares move, not even me.

And then, through the fearsome ring of his troops, appears the hammer of Bruno Gascoyne, the victor of Kingsland Meadow. A frail old man, surely not less than seventy, who leans on an olive-wood stick clearly marked: "A Souvenir of the Holy Land."

"Mr Silkstone, I presume," he says. I stretch out my hand, which he clasps. "Thanks be to God I am still alive," he says. "How the doctors saved me only He knows. You thought I was a crazy old man when we talked on the telephone. Lucky for you I am so crazy!"

I'm about to say he could be as mad as a hatter for all I care when Sharon takes it into her head to create a vacancy at the *Jewish Voice.*

"Before was just a warning," she cries, lunging at me with a carving knife, "this is for keeps!"

"Bruno," I yell, as we sprint around the perimeter, "for God's sake, tell her to stop, before they kill her!"

"Nonsense," replies Gascoyne, "Jews don't do that sort of thing." Sharon discovers otherwise.

Caught in the back by a burst of gunfire she abandons the chase and rolls herself into a ball on the ground, like a hedgehog hit by a car. Tighter and tighter she clasps her knees, as though she were trying to shrink herself back into the womb, until the grip snaps and her limbs, now completely out of control, begin to twitch promiscuously. Her eyes say nothing. She is in the power of a sadist, pleasuring himself in the intimate intricacies of her central nervous system. Finally, his passion spent, the Angel of Death leaves her be, and she slumps on her side and dies.

Adam attempts to cover her with a blanket, but Bruno has more dramatic ideas. He raises his dead daughter and exits with her dangling body in his arms.

"Out of my way," he cries, "you are men of stone!" He strides onward as long as his strength allows; then, bowed down by the weight, he sinks upon all fours. Moonlight illuminates his white streak, emphasizing the blackness of the rest, and as he grows smaller and smaller I have the distinct impression that he is altering his form and changing into his namesake.

Once upon a time the peasantry would take out their hatred for the aristocracy upon the badger, undoubtedly a noble beast. They would throw a captured brock into a cage and pit their best dogs against it until the surrogate gave up the ghost and canine teeth delivered their little triumph. What else has our victory become? Henceforth the badger will be a creature to fear. At all events avoid the jaws, for the lower is so articulated to the upper, by means of a transverse knuckle firmly locked into the cranium, that their hold is unbreakable.

At dawn we send the orphans of Albion and their foreign backers packing. Adam Smith, however, refuses to budge until we have located Sharon's remains. These are discovered beneath a wormy pile of newly dug earth, more fitting for an animal's set than a young woman's last couch. No one objects when Adam proposes to leave her for exhumation centuries hence. We shake hands.

"Give my regards to Lena," he says.

14

"Joshua," shouts Lena, as we enter the house, "Daddy's back!"

And the believer in miracles hugs his answered prayer. I introduce my rescuer. My wife thanks him for forestalling, if only temporarily, the gypsy's curse.

"I was sick with worry about you," she says to me, an echo of the exclusive intimacy we once shared.

Such an extraordinary reunion cannot help but revive our moribund relationship, although it takes an effort to accept that I am really home. When you have considered yourself doomed for any length of time it is hard to see yourself as anything other than a temporary visitor. Even in the arms of your wife and only son it is not your existence but your non-existence that you take for granted. Though, looked at another way, Lena and Joshua confirm the presence of a husband and father. Anyway, we certainly look a family to the rheumy eyes of my saviour.

"Now I see why you were in such a hurry," he says. "Had I such a wife I too would run home. You remind me of Lorna Wingate, Mrs Silkstone. She was a real beauty, ask anyone who knows her. It is quite a coincidence, this resemblance, for Lorna's husband, although long dead, has been with me almost as much as your own these last few hours. If the truth were told you'd have to agree that we owe him everything. In short, Mrs Silkstone, if it wasn't for Orde the Jews would still be stateless and you would be a widow.

"I met him at the beginning of his career, in Palestine, appropriately enough. He had an apartment in the Talbieh district of Jerusalem. You went in, noted the point-to-point trophies, and thought you were in the Home Counties, until you saw the view. The other officers didn't look, because the hills weren't green enough to remind them of England. Orde was a captain in the intelligence, and he was the only one with any, which didn't win him many friends. Except among the Jews, of course.

"I remember when he came up with the idea of the Special Night Squads. Whenever he wore his wolfish grin you could be sure he was concocting a scheme that would scare the pants off his superiors. Most thought he was a dangerous madman. Why, even today the official war historians go out of their way to blacken his name. They say his fertile imagination would form an interesting psychological study! Freud you don't need to be to work out why they hated him. But somehow he managed to persuade those anti-Semites to let the kibbutzniks have some guns. His next job was to convince the Hagana to abandon its policy of *havlaga*. Hitler will kill all the Jews in Europe, he said, so the future of your people is here. If you want to survive you must learn to fight for your lives.

"I was there at Kibbutz Hanita on the historic night when Wingate led the first raid against the Arabs. He was Joshua son of Nun. His eyes, always piercing blue, were like planets. Pistols and grenades hung from his belt. In one hand were wire-cutters, in the other a Bible. His theory was simple: be audacious, be mobile, above all, be a surprise. Well, Mr Silkstone, was I a chip off the old block?"

Taking my cue I retell the story of the night attack, the authorized version, for which Sharon has been resurrected as agreed.

"Now," says the hero, as the tale comes full circle, "it is

time for me to bow out. Temporarily, at least. Jake, when you have rested I want to make you a serious offer. Don't look so alarmed, I have decided to write my own life story. For you I have chosen a winner, a real hero."

That night, in bed, Lena tells me that she loves me, a sentiment unexpressed since the advent of Uzi. On the edge of sleep I suddenly exclaim, "Blast! I forgot to give him Unger's address."

"And I forgot to tell you that Unger phoned here," says Lena. "He left a message. Said he had decided to spare Smolinsky after all. Whatever that means."

The perfect ending. Dozing on my wife's bosom, feeling secure for the first time in months, I decide that none of us must ever leave this house again. Forget about the *Jewish Voice*, forget about Israel, let the three of us shut out the world with its illnesses and dangerous diversions.

IV Jerusalem

1

Every year at Pesach time millions of *pontia daplicide*
cross the Judaean wilderness and enter Jerusalem. White
butterflies girdle the walls of the Old City like an infinitely
long prayer-shawl, one end of which gathers high above
the holy of holies until the evening wind, blowing out of the
desert, scatters it and the sky seems filled with nothing
more than the debris of a political rally. Suddenly the
lepidoptera are overtaken by a force greater than the wind
and are dragged across the heavens as if they were albino
iron filings and the silver skull-cap of the al-Aqsa mosque
were really a giant magnet.

As for the Dome of the Rock, it begins to glow like a
nuclear reactor on heat, turning the congregation of
butterflies suspended above it from a pillar of cloud into a
pillar of fire. But deep within this miraculous portent
unholy deeds are taking place; in short, the *pontia
daplicide* are mating.

To be more frank, the lily-white nimbus is actually an
airborne bordello. The whore of Babylon was a novice
compared to the female butterfly, which raises a few issues
when it comes to the question of paternity, for the males
are as jealous as August Strindberg (whose favourite
creature they were). They have more marbles, however,
and try to retain their sanity, not to mention their genetic
inheritance, by fucking their nympho-wives senseless, for
which purpose they have been blessed with fake ejaculate
which fills the lady's spermatheca to the meniscus. Sated
with love she swoons to the ground, allowing the genuine
sperm to get on with the job of fertilizing her eggs
unmolested, while her punch-drunk mate snoozes on her
wing.

Foolish man, full of self-delusion! For there is yet
another threat to family life in the shape of buccaneer
males who bugger their own sex and regard with ironic

detachment the efforts of the catamite to deposit the wrong sperm into his mate's reproductive system. Lucky is the caterpillar who knows his father!

2

On the same day, in another part of the sky, though with thoughts no less libidinous, I look down upon the purple Aegean, across its crimson corset, and into the awaiting night as if the scene of my next encounter with Hannah Ben-Tur were projected on to that dark future. Would I, this time, have the courage to redeem her promise? Why else was I going to Israel?

I had packed two books for the journey; the famous biography of Orde Wingate by Christopher Sykes and Kafka's *Letters to Friends, Family and Editors.* Browsing through the latter I was forced to consider the possibility that I had not fucked Hannah when I had the chance because I feared that my penis might take it into its head not to perform. It will come as no surprise, I'm sure, to learn that I have never been on particularly good terms with my organs.

We are like (say) the Israelis and the Palestinians, fighting over the same bit of land (still, according to the captain, another hour or so away). The Israelis have an ineradicable advantage. They have a story. So do I. My organs do not, any more than the Palestinians, which pleases neither. Defeat, however, does not necessarily ensure subservience. On the contrary, aggrieved nihilists are more likely to destroy what they cannot own. So the pain begins or the fear of pain or the bombing and shooting. Israel was almost into its second decade before the Palestine Liberation Organization got off the ground; my organs began to terrorize me before I was three (take note, any psychoanalysts who have got this far). Little cramps probed my bowels, my bladder dilated like an over-extended balloon. Instead of supporting me, my parents sided with my organs — "Go to the toilet," being their battle-cry. It was the first skirmish in a struggle that still has not ended: my War of Independence.

In the beginning my tactics were intuitive; I had no inkling of the connection between food and shit, but I knew enough to stop eating. Though I was sufficiently sly to pretend otherwise. Thus I chewed my meals but did not swallow, storing the masticated gobs in my cheeks until I was able to spit them down the lavatory bowl, thereby fooling my parents on two counts. But when an aunt pinched my arm on the beach at Bournemouth and said, "They looked fatter coming out of Belsen," my mother, unaware of the cause of my anorexic condition, made an appointment to see a Harley Street paediatrician.

3

I can no longer describe him, of course, but I shall never forget the transparent homunculus that stood upon his desk. Blue roots descended from the head, inside of which was a grey thing like a curled-up pup, at the tip of whose tail was an unblinking eye. Some of the roots ran down the manikin's arms and legs through rhubarb-coloured clay, but the main one joined a red pipe which was itself connected at the chest cavity to a violet lump. On either side of this crouched speckled dwarves sucking at purple straws. One sat upon a shiny cushion, while the other rested upon a hairless cat with a blank bloody face. Below that a bloated centipede curled blindly around a seething pit of pinkish snakes, beneath which two cephalic tadpoles banged their heads together. As well they might, for between them, looking like the sight of a gun, was a cross-sectioned penis. And the more I think about Hannah, as the flight progresses, the more I feel like that uncocked midget.

Certainly that was how I appeared to the paediatrician with his X-ray eyes. As far as he was concerned I was nothing more than the sum of my organs.

"Good morning, Mrs Silkstone," he boomed. "Let's see it."

My mother, assuming the impersonal pronoun referred to her son, began to undress me.

"Not so fast, Mrs Silkstone," he said, "I'd like to examine his exports first. Did you bring the stool?"

"I'm sorry, Doctor," said my mother, shaking her head, "he hasn't been for more than a week."

"An obstinate bugger," he said. "I don't suppose there's any use asking him to urinate into this?" He offered my mother a flask, which she pushed away. "In that case you'd better strip the little blighter after all," he said.

My mother, as anxious as a stage-struck parent at her child's first audition, unbuttoned my dungarees and delivered me into the doctor's hands. These removed my pants and then, without warning, taped a polythene bag over my genitals and, bending me double, forced a suppository into my anus. It worked within minutes and I stood there utterly humiliated as I surrendered control of my sphincters to my violator.

Ever since that moment my organs have been plotting to repeat their triumph. Nowadays my kidneys are like those scruffy malcontents you see outside urinals selling socialist newspapers, while my liver is even more Bolshevik, dedicated to overthrowing the system altogether. *You're nothing but a running dog of the Zionist, racist, imperialist ruling clique, it grunts; come the day and you'll be put down with the rest of them. Just let a few cancer cells sneak past your fucking antibodies and I'll start the job tomorrow!*

"If I go," I say, "I'll take you with me." *That's what you think, say my kidneys, ever heard of organ transplants?*

It is not pleasant to contemplate a surgeon removing vital organs from your lightly charred corpse, especially when you are suspended 35,000 feet above terra firma, and I begin to fear that my ill-conceived presence will bring disaster to flight LY318. So I labour to replace my mind's lascivious baggage with thoughts of the more earnest endeavours I intend to undertake once we have landed in Israel. I add, "*kayn aynhoreh,*" to ward off the evil eye, my organs' great ally.

How did my mother defend herself when the paediatrician chided her for her superstitious ways?

"I am not a fool, Doctor," she had said, "I know that the evil eye can attack your organs or your luck, and that if it attacks the former it is called a virus. But what of bad luck? What causes that? You won't find the answer under a microscope. When you bring me it I'll stop saying *kayn aynhoreh.*"

I couldn't have put it better myself. Comforted, I return to the lives upon my lap, the Jewish dreamer and the Gentile man of action, both of whom had their own ideas about my destination.

4

I am not naturally gregarious and find no pleasure in conversing with strangers on long journeys, especially when my neighbour turns out to be an elderly German spinster with caged canaries on her lap. Fortunately she has a travelling companion, a stout old Israeli lady with grey curly hair and poor eyesight, to judge from the thickness of her lenses. They had embarked at Frankfurt, where the plane had landed to pick up extra passengers. As they progressed along the aisle, looking like a pair of grotesque miners from a Grimm's fairy tale, the one with her canaries, the other leaning on two canes, I knew that they were destined for the empty seats beside me.

Thus far we have spoken only once. Observing that I preferred not to eat the slices of smoked turkey served for dinner, the German had asked if she could have them for her birds.

"With pleasure," I had replied, and watched with some fascination while her pets queued up religiously to receive the wafer-thin slices of their betters.

Now, however, she seems disconcertingly interested in

the book I am reading, so much so that I can hear her wheezing tubes and feel her phlegmy breath on my cheek. Determined not to give her the opportunity to speak, I close Kafka's *Letters* and leave my seat, hoping to find a hostess wheeling the cocktail trolley. I succeed.

Upon my return I find that an old man has taken my place. Once he was tall, but now his shoulders are stooped, as if he were one of Pliny's wondrous men whose heads grow upon their chests. His hair is white, his eyes are dark. His face is so bony that, for an instant, I have the illusion that those eyes are on the end of stalks shaped like question marks. None the less, he is obviously a more communicative soul than me, for an animated conversation now replaces the silence I left.

"You were always so energetic," he says to the old woman who is clutching her sticks as if she were out of control on slalom run, "what is the matter?"

"My friend has been in hospital in Frankfurt," replies the German, "for major surgery. The doctors have given her a new hip. I am not her nurse exactly, but I have been retained by her son to look after her until she is walking unaided."

"That is as it should be," replies the man.

"Enough, enough," cries the Israeli. "I am overjoyed to see you looking so well after all the stories that I heard. I am happy also that you have decided to come to my country. But, tell me, why has it taken you so long?"

"When you are dead you lose all sense of time," he replies.

"Of course," says the Israeli.

I have not yet been introduced to the interloper, but I cannot resist asking, "What's the point of being a ghost if you still have to travel by aeroplane?" He looks at me with such compassion that I feel ashamed.

"Even the dead are subject to the laws of time and space," he says. "I have not been blessed with disembodiment." His eyes turn luminous with tears.

"Satisfied?" asks the German.

"Please, my little Palestinian," he says, turning his back on me, "tell me why you left without a word? I sent you postcards, but you didn't reply. How did I offend you?"

"My dear friend," replies the old Israeli, "that was nearly sixty years ago. I do not remember."

"Look at him," whispers the German. "Who could blame her? Those European Jews were not exactly *ubermenshen*. I know all about it. He followed her from Prague to Eberswalde in 1923. He looked at her with those big eyes of his as if to say, 'Take me home with you.' Then she became a teacher at the Victoria Heim in Berlin, a boarding school for illegitimate girls, and he turned up there too. Naturally the bastards all assumed the same thing: he was her suitor. She was a young woman at the start of her career. She didn't need a scandal, nor a millstone."

"Do you at least recall the letter I sent you in the Hebrew you taught me? 'Don't laugh,' I wrote in brackets when I had to guess a word. But how could you not laugh? I was under the impression that you were in anxious expectation of a letter from your parents. You told me you could not move to Berlin without their consent. So I tried to comfort you: 'I well understand the panic with which one waits for an important letter which wanders all the time. How many times in my life have I burned with such anxiety? What wonder that a man does not become ashes long before it appears.' But how unlike me you were. Even before I finished writing the letter you were in Germany."

"I was young," replies the Israeli, "and very impatient. I had my own life to lead. I couldn't wait for anyone, neither you nor my parents. I confess that I did not realize that you were a genius, but even if I had it would have made no difference."

"Ah," replies the man, "but that's exactly why I loved you. I loved you because you didn't understand me."

"Of course she understood you," says the German. "Men are not difficult to understand."

"I am talking about my writing," he says. "If you had

understood that, my little Palestinian, you would not have been yourself. You were too healthy, too fearless, too self-confident to have looked twice at my unhealthy scribblings. It was for your vitality that I loved you."

"But look at me now," says the Israeli, "old, crippled. My sticks are made in America. My hip comes from Germany, as does my nursemaid."

"But you have children," says the old man, "a new generation in a new home."

The Israeli woman turns her head away and looks out of the window, as I had done an hour or so ago, in the hope of glimpsing the future. "Look!" she cries. "There are lights on the horizon. We've reached Tel Aviv."

The old man leans across the German with her canaries and presses his face against the Perspex. "I feel like Moses on Mount Nebo," he says.

"Ladies and gentlemen," interjects the captain, "we have just crossed the coastline of Israel. We shall be landing at Ben-Gurion Airport in ten minutes. Please return to your seats and fasten your safety belts. Please extinguish all cigarettes."

"Excuse me," I say, "I'd better do what the pilot wants."

"Of course," says the old man, rising from my seat, "and I must return to my own place."

Having volunteered to help the two women off the plane, I remain in my seat until the cabin is empty. We are making our way slowly toward the exit when we hear the old-fashioned sound of tubercular coughing, and we turn around to see our erstwhile companion lost in a cloud of poisonous fumes left by a group of German tourists who couldn't wait to get at their duty-free cigarettes. The smoke enmeshes him like a silken shroud, turned glassy by his dewy cough. His clothes and skin dissolve into the web, leaving him uprotected against our horrified gaze. Before our eyes are fluttering lungs, hunched like a pair of Rumpelstiltskins over vats of air, but even as we watch they rise and plunge their sharpened straws into the palpitating heart.

"I cannot do it!" cries the fading man. "They will not let me get off the plane."

Two stewards rush to his aid, but there is nothing they can do to revive him.

It takes the old Israeli woman nearly twenty minutes to descend the steps.

"What a fate," I say, "to be condemned to re-enact your death throes every time a plane lands in Israel. Can't the rabbis perform an exorcism or something? I know one who would be willing to have a try."

"You do not understand," says the Israeli woman, squeezing my arm. "He was — how do they call it? — the in-flight entertainment. Other airlines have movies, El-Al has ghosts. Kafka, Celan, Joseph Roth, Stefan Zweig, Bruno Schulz, Miklos Radnoti, to name only the writers-in-residence. Sometimes they give readings. Other times, as was the case this evening, they converse with the passengers. But always the ending is the same. Death. It is not without meaning, as you must realize. Indeed there are non-believers among our people who claim that there are no ghosts at all but holograms, manufactured under licence from Walt Disney. Who can be sure? I am just a poor old teacher. What do I know of these modern gimmicks? All I know is what I have seen with my own eyes. Counterfeit or not, tonight's encounter has brought back many memories and revived an old guilt which is real enough."

When we are settled into the airport bus she continues: "One of his friends, who lived in Jerusalem, persuaded me to go to Prague. It was 1921. I was barely out of my teens, having lived all my life in Palestine. Who could resist such an adventure? His mother approached me upon my arrival and made arrangements for me to teach her son Hebrew. I was the third to try. My predecessor, Professor Thieberger, had been relegated by his father — you know all about him, of course — to a dark room on the other side of the kitchen, which gives you some idea of the status of Hebrew in that household. I was promoted to the dining-room. He was sick all the time, as you have seen, and his mother would peep into the room to make sure that her son was not over-exerting himself. She had reason. He wanted to devour the language. He wanted to know the words for everything, as if he really believed his promise, that he would be in Palestine by the following autumn. More than once he got lost in his own thoughts and he would laugh so much that he would have to lie down on the sofa. Fortunately I already had an attitude to psychology, so I left him alone and didn't say a word. I never really knew what he wanted from me. He was so shy. Sometimes he would make a compliment such as, 'You look so nice today, with your red dress,' just to show me that he knew I was a woman. But usually he remained silent. Whatever it was that he wanted I knew that it was not in me to give to him. In the end I ran away. I didn't even go to see his friend when I came home. That I still feel bad about. But I had my own life to live."

Finally, as we go our separate ways, she says: "I think he loved me as a teacher. But he never touched my hand."

5

Those sentences haunt me as I drive my hired Seat out of the airport in the direction of Jerusalem: "*I think he loved me as a teacher. But he never touched my hand.*" In the fields on either side of the road, tractors with illuminated spotlights move to and fro as if the farmers feared that the fertile soil, jealous of their sleep, would vanish overnight. Having at last gained possession of their own land these Jews are now possessed by it. Like mad things they plant and build and feed it the flesh of their sons and the blood of their neighbours.

My wife is a teacher, and it took some while before I plucked up the courage to touch her hand. But I did, and more, and we have a son to prove it. Since then she has touched home base with others, I regret to say, but that is another chapter. He was tall, attractive to women. So why did he sit on his hands? Because he knew in his heart that Palestine was beyond him? Certainly it lay across a great divide unknown to cartographers. By reaching over the dining-room table and bridging the gap between himself and his Hebrew teacher he would therefore be transgressing holy space. From his point of view, touching hands would have been a blasphemous act, akin to the sin of worshipping the Golden Calf. It would have been to reduce the Promised Land to a lump of flesh, albeit a pretty one. Had he embraced her he could have kidded himself that he had simultaneously taken possession of Palestine. Unthinkable! For him, not me. When it comes to screwing, I am a materialist. And yet it was undeniable that I also didn't "touch" Hannah Ben-Tur when she offered herself, and was called a "cunt-teaser" for my scruples. Scruples! Perhaps the truth of the matter is that I was intimidated by her passport. What could I offer that her warrior-husband couldn't? Peace and quiet, she has subsequently suggested. Very flattering.

6

My ears pop as I begin the ascent through the pine woods that marks the end of the coastal plain and the beginning of the heroic road to Jerusalem. It is a lonely route this late at night and I succeed in convincing myself that out there among the rising sap Hannah's husband or his long dead comrades-in-arms are waiting to teach me my real place in Jewish history, though any expert will tell you that formerly such ambushes were the prerogative of the Arabs. However, it is not one of their number that I want to dishonour and cuckold. Nor do I take personally their threat to murder every visitor they can lay their hands on this Pesach-cum-Easter. Until, that is, the last bridge on the road when I can already sense if not see the still-warm honey-coloured stones of the approaching city. Here, as I change down a gear in anticipation of the steep climb ahead, several men in battle fatigues suddenly step from behind one of the buttresses.

No need to tell you at what target their guns are aimed. Neither do I need to be a semiotician to understand what is required of me. But should I stop? Supposing they are Arab terrorists? But if they are Israelis and I don't stop they'll think I'm a terrorist and shoot me!

I do stop. They are Israelis.

They want to know where I am going, but not why. "Neveh Sha'anan," I tell them, the Vale of Tranquillity. They wish me luck. It is enough for them that I am on their side, which is where I am, when all is said and done. Imbued with patriotic spirit I consider, for only the second time since I took off from Heathrow, the public reason for my journey, which is what I would have told the soldiers, had they asked. My wife believes me, why shouldn't they?

In short, after endless phone calls from the man who rescued me from Bruno Gascoyne, I have agreed to write a life of Wingate. Son of Plymouth Brethren, descendant of distinguished soldiers, the solitary boy was inevitably seduced by the military adventures in the book that was, so his parents said, the literal truth. Sent away to Charterhouse, the young romantic must have fancied himself as Moses at the Court of Pharaoh destined, though no one knew it, to lead his people to the Promised Land. How else to explain this righteous Gentile's infatuation with Zionism? My father certainly could come up with no better answer. Indeed, he seemed peculiarly reluctant to speculate upon why any goy should have such an unnatural interest in Jews, nor did he mellow when I coyly informed him that I intended to put on record, at last, his hitherto unknown role in the creation of Israel. By the end of the book, having followed Wingate through Palestine, Abyssinia and Burma, I was expected by my backer to have provided enough evidence to discredit the denigration of his hero contained in the third volume of the official *History of the Second World War*, concerning the campaign against Japan. For this I will be paid a fee of

£3000 plus expenses, these to include at least one trip to Israel to meet veterans of Wingate's Special Night Squads. It is not a deal that will please my agent, but then she has not yet saved my life.

At the outset my knowledge of strategy was nil, but already I am something of an expert on long-range penetration, Wingate's favoured philosophy. You can imagine with what delight I introduced that phrase into my increasingly passionate correspondence with Hannah Ben-Tur. She had, in fact, complained of a lack of spontaneity in my letters, so I had responded with a virtuoso piece on the theme of Wingate's tactics which was, of course, designed to be an incitement to masturbation. I for one confess that shortly thereafter I committed adultery with my right hand and a pot of Vaseline.

I have also learned the importance of reconnaissance and so instead of going straight to the empty apartment in the German Colony, the property of a friend of my benefactor's, I drive out past the old campus at Givat Ram, in accordance with the map laid out on the passenger seat, and cut down a narrow road beside the Shrine of the Book which looks, in the moonlight, like the amputated breast of a recumbent giantess.

I am now in the Valley of Tranquillity, which is no description of my mood. I continue slowly, driving without lights, until I come to a stop outside the Ben-Tur residence.

Surprise is another of Wingate's axioms. Hence I have not informed Hannah of my plans. She certainly has no idea that I am at this moment sitting in a hired Seat opposite her house and watching, without the benefit of binoculars, the rituals of bedtime.

Having vacant land opposite her room has made her careless and she neglects to pull her curtains, enabling me to watch history repeat itself for a third time as she unbuttons her dress. Tonight her underwear is of the kind you see in glossy magazines, as if my presence were somehow expected. Nor is the way she walks over to her

dressing-table entirely innocent. She examines herself in
the mirror, paying particular attention to her breasts, which
seem magnified by her shiny brassière. Satisfied, she
extracts a letter from one of the drawers. The envelope is
unmistakable. It is one of mine. She removes the sheets of
paper, over which I laboured so long, and makes a tube of
them, as if she were rolling a king-size joint. Next, contrary
to all the rules of strip-tease, she pulls down her pants.
Then, standing with her back to me, her buttocks clasped
in prayer, she begins to rub my words between her thighs.
It is, without doubt, the finest review my work has ever
received.

As I watch her gradually succumb to the pleasures of my
text, the sacred and the profane become impossibly
confused in my mind, hardly surprising, given the
location of my sin.

On previous visits to Jerusalem I had seen the sick, the
superstitious, the religious and the lovelorn, not to
mention the late Moshe Dayan, squeeze prayers penned on
cigarette-like scrolls into the crevices of the Wailing Wall.
Oh, Hannah is my Wailing Wall, my Temple Mount, its
moss and lichen her pubic hair, its crevices the clefts of her
vulva and anus. She is my Temple Mount, and I rise in her
honour. My prayer is for victory; the land, her land, will be
mine. I feel as full of news as the spies Joshua sent to
Jericho. They're welcome to Rahab the harlot. I'm perfectly
happy with Hannah Ben-Tur. I just envy them the moment
when they returned to the encampment at Shittim. I have
no Joshua to report to. Nor even a Wingate. Would that I
had heeded another of his rules — always guard your back.

For my passenger door opens and a familiar figure lowers
himself upon the map of Jerusalem and its environs.

"Jesus Christ," I say, "what are you doing here?"

His interpretation of "here" is more geo-political than
my intention:

"I got an invitation to Israel after all, no thanks to our
deceased friend. On the contrary, it came from Shalom
Acshav. Fortunately my government had second thoughts.

They gave me permission to come. So here I am."

"I meant, what are you doing outside Hannah's house in the middle of the night?"

"Ah," he says, "it is the consequence of a happy coincidence. As luck would have it, Mr Ben-Tur is one of the leaders of Peace Now. So I have been able to give Mrs Ben-Tur further details of her grandfather's history, as well as put her in touch with several members of her family still resident in Poland. The Ben-Turs are a most hospitable couple."

"I can see how well you are repaying them," I observe.

"My dear friend," he says, "you are very naïve."

Then I remember — as if I had ever forgotten — Ziz's penchant for up-market whorehouse lingerie, and I realize, with a mixture of anger and embarrassment, that I am a gatecrasher at a performance meant for one.

"Have you fucked her?" I ask, realizing with a shock that I will forgive his adulteration of my wife if he will only say no. I am even prepared to accept a lie.

"Of course not," he says. "Your wife is one thing. Your mistress quite another." Unfortunately I am in no position to punch him in the eye for that low blow. "She is saving herself for you," he says. "I begged her to use any of my poems, but she insisted upon your epistle. She is a prosaic woman, I'm afraid."

By now Hannah has worked her way through the alphabet down to O. Her body seems to be dividing itself into two; from the waist up she is petrified, the veins and sinews clearly visible in her neck, but down below her hips twist as though they wanted to break free and live a life of their own. Before that can happen, however, Hannah's husband suddenly enters the picture.

"She is saving herself for him too, I regret to say," remarks Ziz. "Can you give me a lift?"

I drop him outside the King David Hotel.

"You are sure you don't want a nightcap?" he asks.

"Positive," I say. His presence has unsettled me. I must make new plans. What would Wingate have done?

I am back at Neveh Sha'anan just after the dawn of the following day. At seven-thirty her four children emerge with their blue back-packs, kiss their mother goodbye, and wander hand-in-hand down the road toward the local school. Hannah, in her nightdress, watches them until they become four dots among many.

An hour passes. Still her husband has not departed. I am beginning to worry. It is imperative that I see her before Ziz has the chance to telephone and spoil my surprise, hence my early sortie. I know that any delay in resuming where we left off in my office will disturb my momentum to such an extent that I won't be able to go on. Indeed, I am seriously considering a tactical withdrawal when her front door opens. There is now no one between me and the goal.

"Shoot!" cries the crowd.

I knock. The door opens.

"You!" cries Hannah. I encircle her with my arms. "You're crazy," she says. "What if my husband were here?"

"I saw him leave," I say. "I've been sitting in my car outside your house for the best part of three hours."

"You must be stiff," she says.

"Feel," I say.

"You're positive this time?" she asks. I nod. "In that case," she says, "there is something I must tell you."

"I know all about Ziz," I say. She looks at me, astonished.

"Please," I say, "no more talking. Already I'm getting visions of rapists and child molesters, buggers and burglars, germs and viruses, cars and lorries, all drawing lots to see who's going to get my wife and child."

"If you're sure," says Hannah.

"To tell you the truth," I say, "I'm really frightened that it won't stay up. I don't want to disappoint you after such a long engagement."

Blood Libels

"I won't be the one who's disappointed," says Hannah, "I can promise you that much."

She leads me to her bedroom, which I have already seen from the outside.

"Draw the curtains," I say. She looks at me. "I know about that too," I say.

In the twilight world of her room she removes her dress yet again. Her underwear is more simple today, just a bra and pants. I have nothing left but my briefs.

"You first," says Hannah.

"You've got more to hide than me," I protest. Actually I am trying to conceal the fact that detumescence has set in.

"Very well," she says. Now the mere idea of her pubic hair is normally enough to send me crazy with lust, but its physical presence is another matter. Nothing stirs. "I'm ready," says Hannah, reaching out to remove my pants.

"Not yet," I say.

We embrace and exchange tongues, anything to defer the moment of truth. I caress her back. I fumble with the catch on her brassière.

"Don't," she says.

"I want to see your breasts," I say.

"You can't," she says, which I take to be a tease. It isn't. It's a statement of fact. Bra-less Hannah steps back. She is right. I can't see her breasts — because there is only one. A breast in the singular. It — the right one — is perfect, but where the left breast should have been is only puckered skin, slightly shiny with radiation burns, and the scar of an operation.

"Satisfied?" she sobs. "Now you know. I've had a fucking mastectomy. I warned you. This goddam country has turned me into an Amazon. Now put on your clothes and go away."

Too true, I'd like nothing better than to get on the next plane home. But I cannot, in all conscience, leave Hannah like this. I bend and kiss the wound. I kneel and kiss her cunt. My tongue touches her salty epithelium. She sighs.

138

"Lie down," I say.

"On my front?" she asks.

"No," I say, "on your back." And I stand before her supine body naked, fearless. Such is the perversity of my desire that penetration is no longer a problem. "Consider yourself touched," I say, as I enter her.

"Well," she says, "is it so terrible? Has the sky fallen on you?"

"It's not me I'm worried about," I reply.

"Forget your wife," she says, "at least while we're doing it. I'm sure she'd prefer it that way."

So I begin to move, inside Hannah. Often, when we are pleasuring ourselves in the conjugal bed, I look down upon Lena's breasts and imagine that their nipples are the sightless eyes of a captive who must dance to my tune. Naked, defenceless, they provoke me beyond reason.

Out of the question with Hannah, of course.

Instead, recalling what she did to me in my office, I slide my finger between her vagina and bum, until it is moist enough to squeeze up her anus, so far that I can feel myself on the other side of the membrane. Whereupon Hannah locks her arm around my neck and presses her lips against my ear. I feel her tongue exploring, exploring, until she has my lobe. So hard does she bite it that I involuntarily force myself deeper into her insides.

"You faggot," she hisses, "the more I hurt you the more you like it. Make me come, you faggot!"

Perhaps this is the point of no return, the moment when I reach that invisible line between responsibility and selfishness, beyond which everything will be tainted because of that instant when I was prepared to put all at risk. I am in no state to judge. Here because of weakness I marvel at the new-found strength that has forced the woman beneath me to abandon control of her body. The words that stream into my ear from her overheated mouth are no longer coherent — "Yes yes fuck me you bastard harder harder harder yes yes give it to me fuck me fuck me fuck me rub me in it rub me in it rub me out oh God I'm

coming Jake Jake Jake I'm coming fuck me you bastard oh
God oh Jake. . . ."

Breathless I reach the border crossing where the officials
demand to see my documents, which I don't have. "You
must go back " they say. But it's too late. I cannot stop. "I'm
coming whether you like it or not," I cry. And I enter Israel.

8

It is a divided country. In the post-coital prattle that
accompanies diurnal copulation Hannah describes her
husband's metamorphosis from an indifferent supporter of
nationalistic policies into an obsessive peacenik. It
reminds me of other transformations: of mine — from
cuckold to adulterer; of my wife's — from teacher to
courtesan.

"He was in favour of the invasion at first, you know.
After poor Uzi got shot in London he was all for giving the
bastards a bloody nose. He got blood all right, but he also
got converted. On *Derech Damascus*, the Damascus road,
no less. That much you've read in my letters. Would you
like to know the details?

"Well, it was after a skirmish, when his unit took a few
prisoners. Palestinians. PLO for sure, not nice men. 'Hey,
Ami,' says his sergeant, 'coming with me to the canal?'
Ami thinks he is joking — 'This is 1982 not '67,' he says.
But it's no joke. 'The canal is where we make conversation
with our guests,' explains the sergeant.

"Ami follows him into an abandoned field, where some
soldiers are planting a new crop. They have dug a shallow
ditch, a meter wide and ten meters long. Four prisoners are
in it, head to toe. Face up. They are screaming, holding out
pictures of their wives and kids. Like you would be doing.
They probably think they are already in their graves.
'Fuckers,' shouts a young soldier, 'repeat after me — Yasir
Arafat is an arse-fucking faggot.'

"I know someone who's not a faggot," says Hannah,
interrupting her husband's story in order to place her hand

upon my balls. "You didn't mind me calling you that, did you? I get carried away, which is the whole point, of course.

"Anyway, the Palestinians all curse Arafat. They probably mean it, too. 'Now,' says another soldier, 'we would like some information.' Undoubtedly the Palestinians tell them all they know, but it isn't enough. Yasir Arafat's private telephone number wouldn't have been enough for the sergeant and his little gang that afternoon. 'Right,' he tells the men, 'we'll have to loosen their tongues.'

"How do you loosen a man's tongue? By jumping on his face. In the army they do not wear plimsolls. You can imagine. This is too much for Ami. 'You're crazy men!' he shouts. 'You'll damage their brains.' 'They don't need any,' laughs the sergeant, 'they're Arafat's pawns.' 'Get those men out,' says Ami. He is a captain. They have to obey him. Besides, he is pointing his MK-16 at them. I think it was the most shocking day of his life, more shocking even than when he found out I was sleeping with his best friend.

"Since then, as you know, he has only one thought: to get Israel out of Lebanon. For that he slaves harder than our ancestors in Egypt. *Shalom acshav, shalom acshav*, that's all we hear in this house. That and my screams.

"What's the date today?"

"March 28," I reply. "You should be out burning the hametz, instead of the candle at both ends."

"Forty-seven days since I found the lump," she says. "I'm in the bathroom. The morning shower taken. I look at myself in the mirror. I like what's there. You know what I am thinking? I am thinking, *I wish Jake could see me now.* Remember that dream you described in one of your letters? Well, I follow your instructions faithfully. I touch my thighs and my belly and my breasts. And then I scream.

"No response from downstairs. So I run to the kitchen. I'm stark naked, you'll recall. Ami is there, his nose in *The Jerusalem Post*. 'Mummy has forgotten to put her clothes on,' says my eldest. 'She's dripping all over the floor,' says the youngest. 'I bet there's another scorpion in the sink,' say the twins. Ami still doesn't look up.

"It is Wedenesday, 9 February. The day the final report of the Kochan Commission of Inquiry into the Events at the Refugee Camps in Beirut was published. The whole thing is printed in a special supplement to the paper. 'Ami,' I say, 'I just screamed. Don't you want to know why?' 'Later,' he says.

"It is wonderful to have a husband so concerned with the moral health of his nation, but when you've discovered you may have cancer you do require a little personal interest. 'I need to speak to you,' I say, 'now.' 'What could be more important than the Report?' he asks. So I tell him.

"Our doctor, a friend, sends me straight away to hospital. The following day they operate. 'If it's malignant,' I say, 'let me die.' It is. They don't. I wake up to find Ami in tears. He kisses me. 'I'm sorry,' he says. 'Why are you crying?' I whisper. 'For me?' 'For you,' he says, 'and for Emil.' 'Who's Emil?' I ask. 'Has he got cancer too?' 'He's dead,' Ami replies. 'Someone threw a grenade at our demonstration. A Jew. We ask for peace and they give us bombs. What's happening to us, Hannah?'

"At that moment, I confess, I was more interested in what had happened to me. My left arm looked like an eggplant, that's all I knew. Later they tell me they've taken it all away, from the mammalia to the axilla. I am in the ward two weeks. Then they send me home with a padded bra. 'You'll be able to lead a normal life,' they assure me. 'In Israel?' I say. 'You must be joking.' Now for the punch line."

Hannah pauses. "If it wasn't for you, Jake, I'd be dead today. You saved my life. You and your letters."

Wow! My defeat of Thanatos makes the fabrications to come seem like small change. But it is the kind of recommendation, alas, that will never see the light of day. "Jake Silkstone's writing is like the kiss of life," Hannah

Ben-Tur. Forever secret, unless I want to administer the kiss of death to my marriage.

Come to think of it, Hannah's is the third life my silver tongue has saved. First there was Unger's Smolinsky, then my own, that night in Kingsland Meadow. On the other hand, I have been responsible for several near fatalities — my parents, to name but two — and a couple of actual ones. I have never spelled it out to a soul, but I have this guilty feeling that if I hadn't published my interview with Bruno Gascoyne his daughter wouldn't be a bloodless corpse, nor would there be a fund at the *Jewish Voice* for the unborn child torn from the cooling womb of his murdered mother. There is blood as well as ink upon that other hand.

I suspect that I do not have to tell you what is on Hannah's, which has remained *in situ* since the beginning of her monologue.

"Jake," she says, "I want you to bum-fuck me."

"What for?" I ask.

"Because," she says, "because I want to be filled with life. Death has invaded my body, and I want to fight it at every entrance, even at the one — especially at the one — that leads to the filth that my foe breeds upon."

Thus begins a life or death struggle that requires as much pre-planning as the invasion of Lebanon.

Hannah kneels. "You'll find a dildo in the cupboard beside the bed," she says, "you can use it to open me up, if you like."

"Have you done this before?" I ask.

"No," she replies. "You?"

"No," I say, "I'm scared of catching AIDS."

"So wash your hands afterwards," she says.

Here goes. I smother my finger with K-Y and slide it up as far as my knuckle. Hannah groans, and I get a whiff of that animal smell that just isn't there when you fuck face to face.

The dildo glistens with its artificial lubricant as I introduce it to the bud in Hannah's backside. It is accepted, little by little. Hannah yelps. I stop.

"Don't stop," she insists. So I push harder and the sphincters give way to acommodate the full circumference of the dildo.

"How does it feel?" I ask.

"What do you think?" says Hannah. "Like I'm having a shit."

"You're sure you want to go on?" I ask.

"Yes," she says. "And you?"

"I'm curious," I say.

The skin around her anus is now stretched so tight that it begins to split along the seam at its base. Immediately a thin red line of blood forms.

"You're bleeding," I say.

"Do it," she says.

So I do.

I grasp her shoulders and plug myself into the tail-end of her digestive system. By now it must be nearly mid-morning. We are wet from our exertions and the heat of the room. Hannah's pores drip sweat which collects in the crease between her buttocks, salting my penis as it performs its second good deed of the day. Where it leads I can follow in mind only. I see swamplands swarming with shadowy shapes. I hear their whispered plans to over-throw the body politic and to replace it with an estate after their own image. In short, they are conspiring to kill the woman I love. Love? Where did that word come from? No time for that now. I press on, faster and faster. I've got to save Hannah, to take revenge for all the humiliations I have suffered since that day I was raped by Dr Homunculus. Hannah gasps as my surrogates hit her tubes, eager to eradicate the terrorists. We drop to the floor, lost to society, blood from the conflict staining the rug.

We must have dozed off because the next thing I know is the sound of a kid downstairs. Still in a daze, I think it's Joshua who's calling me. Then I see Hannah and know it isn't. At least I pray to God it isn't. I believe telepathy, though I wish I didn't. The dirtiest trick God ever pulled was to visit the sins of the fathers on the heads of their sons. *Leave Joshua out of this,* I mutter. The response is a sickening premonition. I want a telephone.

"Don't move," says Hannah, putting on her brassière and a wrap, "I'll give him some money for ice cream."

In her absence I get dressed, wondering as I step into my briefs what bacteria are about to take up residence therein. Hannah returns.

"How are you going to explain these to your husband?" I ask, pointing to the incriminating marks.

"No problem," she replies. "I'll say my period caught me on the hop. I'm more interested in what you said to your wife. How *did* you explain this trip? I am why you came, aren't I?"

"That's our secret," I say. "Officially I've come to do research for a book about Orde Wingate. It's a commission. My sugar-daddy has supplied me with a list of kibbutzniks who fought with him. The idea is to interview as many as possible."

"Is Dov Yemina on it?" she says.

"How did you know?" I say.

"Mr Silkstone," she says, "today is certainly your lucky day. You have killed two birds with one stone. Ami has become friendly with Dov through Peace Now. He is a lovely man. In fact he is joining our Seder tonight. So must you."

I say no but am easily persuaded otherwise.

I am as happy as Newton must have been when he twigged why the pippin bopped him on the cranium. What a discovery: personalized gravity, making the world amenable to my desire. Me? A man of action, in control of my destiny? Oh, yes! There is, after all, a pattern, a discernible link between wish and fulfilment, which resembles that diagram concerning the conduction of heat I copied from the blackboard into my exercise book during a physics lesson more than two decades ago. You'll recall that eleven pin men, representing molecules, are standing in a line. The first one, the goalkeeper, catches the ball.

Desire. It is too hot to handle. He throws it to the nearest defender, who passes it to the next, and so on, until it reaches the centre-forward, who blasts it towards the opposing goal. Such is his magnetism that even the opposing goalie has to hug him. There is no doubt, as soccer players are wont to say in another context, that I've scored with Hannah. But there is also this nagging uncertainty with regard to the consequences of my action, for in my drawing the ball disappears off the page and it's impossible to tell whether anyone else got burned by it.

"I know what you're thinking," says Hannah. "You can phone from here if you like."

"No," I say, "I'd rather do it from my place."

We embrace. My hand glides beneath the empty cup of her brassière. The Aztecs used to tear the living hearts out of their captives. Hannah's seems anxious to save them the trouble. *Lub-dub*, it goes, *lub-dub*, as though it were about to break through the over-stretched skin.

"Till this evening," she says.

9

The air, as it often does in the valleys of Jerusalem, smells like a spice cake has just been baked. My car, standing in direct sunlight, feels as if it served as the oven. I open all the windows but the low-latitude air is stricken with post-noon lassitude.

Not so all the people on the hill above Ruppin Street. The road's long leisurely curves allow sporadic sightings of their gangling march toward the Knesset. They are the supporters of the disgraced Minister of Defence, forced from office by the Kochan Commission's conclusion that he was morally responsible for the Beirut massacre, their battle-cry being: "Dom Arov –– Dom Arov — *Melech Yisroel!*" Dom Arov, King of Israel? God forbid!

Banners float over their heads like balloons in a comic-strip. Their contents are no less ferocious: "Death to the PLO, death to traitors!"

More congenial are the reserve troopers and their friends camped outside the President's house. No placards, just a blackboard leaning against a wall, with two sets of figures: y hundred on the left, x thousand on the right. A duster hangs over a peg, for new casualties must be chalked up daily.

It is easy to find an organic equivalent for the first group of splenetic demonstrators, but where in the body will you find a representative of those other conscientious objectors? The heart, perhaps. And where does the fear that is spooking my elation have its niche? Can you answer that, Dr Homunculus?

More to the point, my wife answers the telephone when at last I call her from the apartment on Dor Vedorshav. Yes, everyone is fine!

"Guess who I bumped into?" I say.

"Haven't a clue," she says.

"Ziz," I say.

Into the long silence that follows I read a readmission of infidelity, which more than justifies my own.

"How is he?" she asks.

"He hasn't changed," I reply.

"And you?" asks Lena.

"I haven't changed either," I lie.

I do not divulge either of the day's great discoveries, the second and most recent being that orbits are constant, irrespective of whether the controlling body is contemplating its satellites. You don't believe me?

Consider this experiment. A woman A and a man B, married but not to each other, were connected together. According to the old theory, this should have caused immediate damage to the missing spouses C and D, or even to their offspring E, F, G, H and J. The evidence that the latter all continued unwittingly about their business, despite the fact that their lodestar was temporarily removed, strongly suggests that there is no causal connection between the attraction of A to B and the separate activities of C, D, E, F, G, H and J. It is therefore possible to speculate that if the sun were to vanish from our lives we would be cold, but the world would keep on turning.

As if to confirm this supposition, Lena informs me that it is raining in England. Our disembodied voices flit across the Mediterranean and European terra firma, underpassing oceans or overflying islands. Islands we ain't, that's still agreed, but we seem to have become independent states. In other words, I'm a free man. Except for a new thought, come to tease me. If all retribution were immediate there would be no such thing as irony, my bread and butter.

10

There is much merriment at the Seder table when Ami reaches the paragraph which begins, "The Torah (in commanding the father to tell his children about the Passover) speaks about four kinds of sons — a clever son," he points at the oldest, "a wicked son," he points at the next in line, who pokes his tongue out, " a dull son and one who is too young to ask any questions about the things he sees," he points at the twins, though one is a girl.

Naturally I identify with the wicked son.

"What does the wicked son say?" reads Ami. "He says, 'What does all this service mean to you?' Now because he says 'to *you*', he shows that *he* has no interest in the Seder service. This is a very serious thing, for it means that he separates himself from all the rest of the people of Israel. Therefore the father should give him a sharp answer and say in the words of the Bible: 'It is because of that which the Lord did for me when I came forth out of Egypt.' The father should add this explanation: 'For *me*, and not for *you*; had you been in Egypt, God would not have thought you fit to become a free man.' "

So much for *my* freedom. In furthering the ideology of individual development I have, it would seem, cut myself so far apart from the community of Zion that I would not have found redemption from Egypt. I would have remained, if you like, a slave to my passions. What a paradox! In loving my Israeli I have effectively debarred myself from the rest of the land. But isn't that why she loves me — because I'm not an Israeli? In Kafka's time they weren't interested in weakling writers from the diaspora; now they can't get enough of us — because they think we're sane!

"There is no doubt," says Ami Ben-Tur, "that we are suffering from collective madness. So tonight, before we visit the plagues upon Egypt, let us remove the poison from our own hearts."

He dips a finger into his cup of red wine and lets the drips fall on the tablecloth. For a second I panic. Does he know? Has he sussed the meaning of those other red stains upstairs? Has Hannah confessed? But he is referring, of course, to the bombing of Lebanon and its aftermath.

"An end to war," he says. "Peace now."

Then he dips his finger a further ten times, and we do likewise, repeating after him: "Blood, frogs, lice, wild beasts, pestilence, boils, hail, locusts, darkness and *makat b'horot*, the death of the first-born."

Those words! I can hardly bear to hear them. As one of the unredeemed, would I have been permitted to smear the blood of a lamb on the lintel? Or would the Angel of Death have swooped down upon my innocent kid? How I long to hear those comforting words at the end of *Had Gadya*: "Then came the Holy One, blessed be He, and destroyed the Angel of Death."

But, like that Angel, we have much to devour before we get to the singing, by which time the sweet wine will have made us all tipsy.

"*Shulhan oreih*," says Ami, readjusting his knitted skull-cap and pushing aside his ornate Haggadah, decorated with bird-headed Jews in the style of the anonymous Master of Magentza, "the meal is served."

Hannah and her four children oversee the dinner. Ami, seated at the head of the table, is served first. He slices the peeled and shiny egg, symbol of new life, with a silver spoon of European origin, which just about sums it all up. Passover is back where it began, in the Middle East. *L'shanah haba-ah biryerushalayim*, Next Year in Jerusalem, no longer a dream. At the same time the original issues, centuries dormant in their strange domicile, have been revived. Israel was in Egypt, now it's in Lebanon. And Ami, among many others, is saying — to his own government, it is true — "Let my people go!"

He is a handsome man, which is neither here nor there, but he is also admirable. I am not without shame and felt distinctly unworthy when he welcomed me to his home and introduced his children, all of whom bore his curly-headed stamp.

"My wife has told me much about your work," he said.

Ziz, already present, winked. This made me feel less of a pariah until I realized that I had become the accomplice of my wife's seducer. And I saw myself in years to come as a powdered old pandar, addicted to mascara and rouge, the black and the red, given to pinching my son's wife while my own is ravished by young bucks behind my back. As for my mind, that will be entirely given over to inventing lascivious party games, writing being beyond the abilities of my softened brain.

But no one else sees Ziz as I do. To them he is a righteous Gentile, the great hope of Polish poetry. To me he is a duplicitous bastard. I admit without hesitation the subjectivity of this view. Generally I will not dismiss a writer simply because he is a philanderer. Indeed, it confers superficial glamour, especially if he comes from the puritanical East. But if Ziz was prepared to betray my hospitality why should he stop there, why not also my secrets to the State? You cannot worship a man you do not trust. Of course Ami could say the same about me. My only defence is that I have never been his hero.

No, his champion is Dov Yemina, who certainly looks the part. For a start he appears considerably younger than his seventy years. His sunburned face is kind, though his hair is steely grey, and he sports a fierce white moustache. His shirt, of course, is open at the neck. He wears jeans and leather sandals. The uniform of that archetypal Israeli hero, the soldier-farmer. His real uniform is that of a Lieutenant Colonel in the reserves. Or rather *was*.

At the beginning of March, just over three weeks ago, he published, without benefit of military censorship, his *Diary of the Lebanon War*. It caused a sensation which became a scandal when he received a letter from the military authorities informing him, without explanation, that he was, as of that moment, in retirement.

"For fifteen years since I was discharged from the army because of my age I have been a volunteer," says Dov. "I still am."

"I know the feeling, my friend," says Ziz. "I get banned for supporting Israel, you get the boot for doing the opposite. Maybe we should exchange citizenships." Ziz has a point.

"In a democracy the politicians in power may believe that they personify the nation," says Ami, "but the electorate is always there to remind them otherwise. They are actors and we write the play. In Poland, with respect, they do both. You have no say in the matter. We in Peace Now — and I hope I speak for Dov — will never leave so long as we can show the world that not all the Jews in Israel are Dom Arov types."

I couldn't have put it better myself!

After the eggs comes golden bouillon served in Hannah's dowry. Years before, in Cracow, her grandmother had finally persuaded her husband, old Abe Ratskin, that the merest hint of ostentation might connect them in the minds of their potential persecutors with nouveau-riche *ostjuden*. Thus convinced, he had arranged for their most precious possessions to be safely packed up in an ancient tea chest and shipped off to his brother in Palestine, who subsequently rescued their only son — Hannah's father — from the monastery which had sheltered him during the worst years of the war.

Blood Libels

The crate turned up in Tel Aviv a decade later, giving them all a glimmer of hope, until they saw the date on the yellowing copy of *Gazeta Krakowski* that had been used to wrap the gold-plated dinner-service Hannah resurrects every Pesach.

"It is a miracle," says Ziz, "that I am eating off these plates again. Hannah, this is a wonderful meal, but when I look at it I see instead a Polish goose roasted to perfection by your grandmother, and served on her best crockery with chopped liver, roast potatoes, stuffing and cabbage. Poets, as you are aware, have to endure a period of starvation, especially in their early years. Abe Ratskin, who knew nothing about art, respected my determination to complete my apprenticeship, but insisted that I had at least one meal a week. Friday nights he took me to his home where Shaindel, your grandmother, would be decked out like the shabbat bride, ready to feed our appetites. Afterwards we would rest in front of the open fire — all my memories are of winter — and Shaindel would sit at Abe's feet until her bosom began to glow as red as the coal (your grandmother was a passionate woman, she wore her dresses cut low) and I knew it was time for me to go."

Ziz's reminiscence has scattered our thoughts, sent them in pursuit of our own lost ancestors (not to mention Lena and Joshua, dining tonight with my parents) who lived and died God knows where, but who all, on this selfsame day in the Hebrew calendar, joined in a Seder service. The comfort afforded by this continuity, however, vanishes as soon as Ziz opens his mouth again.

"Not even Abe, a calculating man, had anticipated the ferocity of the whirlwind the Nazis were about to unleash upon the Jews," he says. "Within a very few months the whole neighbourhood was blown apart as if it were a shanty town rather than a solid, respectable area with brick-built houses and tree-lined streets. Who could have guessed? And who would have thought that a couple of generations later my government, among many others, would dare to call *you* — of all peoples — Nazis?"

"Listen," says Dov, "if the Pope himself dropped a bomb it would also kill people. It is not the deed itself but the response we must consider. Unlike my friend here, I was opposed to the war from the beginning, from before the beginning. As soon as we realized what Arov was up to we tried to arrange a demonstration by the inhabitants of Galilee, but we didn't manage to finish the organization because we were called to the banner, as they say. I know Arabic so I was attached to a military government unit that was prepared to follow the fighting troops and take over the tasks of the civilian authorities. Of course in the war the title of 'military government' was erased from our name, because we weren't fighting the Lebanese. Instead they called us the Unit for Help to the Civilian Population. That's why I went, because I was sure that I could do the job of helping the victims better than anyone else, or at least I wanted to. That's why I held on, although I knew that the army was making a big mistake and that my unit wouldn't be much better. And I was right, so I decided: *this time* (I was there in '78, too), *this time I'm not going to keep calm, this time I will write down every detail and publish it afterwards* — the terrible bombardment, the shelling, the killing and the destruction which was sheer brutality. And I published, despite the fact that no 'honourable' publisher would touch my book. It is true that I have been called a traitor, but many others have praised me. I do not think a Nazi officer would have survived very long had he done such things."

"Jake," says Ami, as Hannah brings in the main dish, "what do people think of us in England?"

"Oh," I say, "one holocaust cancels another. So it's open season on the Jews again. Not that anything has actually happened. It's just a mood that's in the air. As for your co-religionists, they've convinced themselves that what they saw with their own eyes was, in reality, Arab propaganda."

"That's why Dov's book is so important," says Ami, helping himself to a chicken breast.

"There are things that must not be forgotten," says Dov. "For instance on 18 June 1982 we had a meeting of senior officers of our unit which was also attended by the **Minister designated as Co-ordinator of Activities for Aid and Restoration of the War Refugees. He was quite** generous about the Lebanese, generous in mouth, but when someone asked about the Palestinian refugees, his immediate reply was, 'Let them go East.' I copied it down on the spot. A friend of mine, a Member of the Knesset, to whom all the time I wrote saying that something terrible is going on up here, raised a question — 'What has the Minister to say about Yemina's story?' Do you know what he replied? 'I need not answer this psychiatrically disturbed person.' I returned my campaign ribbon, but that is a decoration to be proud of."

"Dov has managed to collect enough money to rebuild the school at Ein El-Hilwe camp," says Hannah, carefully biting the flesh off a drumstick. "He was going up to the North once a week until the shooting started again."

"And I would have continued," says Dov, "but the authorities said, 'It is too dangerous to endanger Jewish lives for the sake of those bastards, and anyway we have done enough for them.' They said '*we*', not '*you*'. They were impudent enough to claim that the help came from the government!"

Such distinctions only matter to *us*. It wouldn't have made the slightest difference to Rameses or Hans Frank if the Wicked Son or Abe Ratskin had spoken of their fellow Hebrews as *you* or *we*, as far as they were concerned every Jew was the same, an *it*.

Such speculations don't concern the very young, even in Israel. Noticing that her children are growing restless, Hannah whispers something in her husband's ear and Ami claps his hands and shouts, "Right, my children, it's *tzafun* time; go find it!"

And the four of them leap from their chairs and set to work to uncover the missing piece of matzoh — the *afikoman* — in a way that must be all too familiar to Ziz.

They look in every drawer of the modern black-wood chest (upon whose shiny surface stands the last of the Ratskin silver), under the table, under the seats, in the sofa, even behind the pictures. Shalom of Safed's primitive portrait of Jonah and the whale reveals nothing, but when the younger of the twins lifts Yosl Bergner's *Ascension* away from the wall the matzoh drops out.

The painting catches my eye. At the bottom of the canvas a group of bird-faced Jews, like the ones in Ami's Haggadah, are clustered around a table, in a pose borrowed from a Renaissance master of religious art, but the object of their adoration or astonishment is neither the Lord nor even a minion but a giant turkey, wings extended, on its way to heaven.

Meanwhile the winner hugs her mother and receives her prize, a copy of the *Birds of Israel*, as her smiling father breaks up the *afikoman*, the last piece of matzoh, and distributes it among us all. To look at them now you would think: *Here is a happy family*. But if that were the case there would be no audience, for I should not be present. No, the happy mother kissing her children and her husband has another man's sperm floating around her insides and maybe worse in her glands, while the proud father is on the verge of a nervous breakdown.

However, the image is so persuasive that I doubt my own memory and I begin to wonder whether what I have already described to you is nothing more than a figment of my imagination. Fortunately some of those events are historically verifiable. I could hardly have invented the invasion of Lebanon, could I?

11

We drain the third cup of wine and Ami recites the following prayer, found only in the prayer books of progressive Jews: "How many images this moment brings to mind, how many thoughts the memory of Elijah stirs in us! The times when we were objects of distrust, when our doors were open to surveillance, when ignorant and hostile men forced our doors with terror!"

"May the All-Merciful send us Elijah the Prophet," we respond, "to comfort us with tidings of deliverance."

"Elijah opens up for us the realm of mystery and wonder," continues Ami. "Let us now open the door for Elijah!" Elijah, the scourge of Baal, who was carried to heaven in the very chariot of fire that Bruno Gascoyne demanded — but didn't get — at Kingsland Meadow.

As we listen with our grown-up nonchalance to the other twin unlock the front door to admit the prophet — the symbolic act being his consolation prize — we chant:

"Behold, I will send you Elijah the prophet, and he will turn the hearts of the parents to the children and the hearts of the children to the parents before the coming of the great and awesome Day of the Lord!"

"*Abba, ima*," comes a small voice from the hall, "someone's there!"

A soldier, not dressed for dinner, enters the dining-room. Hannah's face goes white, as if her illness had returned.

"It's him," she whispers to me, "Ami's sergeant, the one I told you about."

"What are you doing here? What do you want?" demands Ami.

"Same answer to both questions," says the sergeant, snapping his fingers: "you."

Two more soldiers enter, Ami's son between them. I notice, for the first time, that all three have a tiny skull embroidered on the flap above the pocket on their army shirts, a death's head where the heart should be.

"What's so important that it can't wait till tomorrow?" asks Hannah. "Is there a mobilization? Where's the war?"

"The war's right here, lady," says the sergeant, "in this room. It's a war between Jews. If you're not for *us*, you're with *them*. And if you're with them you're our enemy. And what do we do to our enemies, before they can do it to us?

We kill them. Forgive the bluntness, Mrs Ben-Tur. A soldier's simple logic."

"I don't believe this," says Ami.

"You'd better," says the sergeant. "If you don't step into the yard pronto we'll shoot you here, in front of your children. We'd rather not. It's more like an execution the other way. Besides, my Yemenite friends are very excitable. Their bullets have a habit of straying. You have some fine pictures, not to mention some pretty faces, in this room. It would be a shame to spoil them."

"Pardon me," says Ziz, "but I was under the impression that Jews didn't kill Jews."

"What? Are you anti-Semitic or something?" raves the sergeant. "Arabs kill Arabs, Indians kill Indians and no one bats an eyelid. Why shouldn't we have the same right?"

"When you put it like that," says Ziz, "I have to agree."

"You are a disgrace to the uniform," says Dov, "nothing but filth. Death squads in Israel! You'd better kill me too. I didn't give the army over forty of my years to build a new Guatemala."

"You're Dov Yemina, aren't you?" asks the sergeant, taking a gulp from Elijah's cup.

"I am," Dov replies.

"In which case," says the sergeant, "it will be a pleasure. Shall we?" He motions with his hand toward the French windows.

"Ami!" Hannah screams. "Don't go like a sheep. Do *something!*"

Ami shrugs.

"Wait!" cries Hannah. "This man is a reporter."

She is pointing at me. Betrayed again!

"So we'll shoot him too," sings the sanguinary sergeant. "Journalists are bastards. They all deserve to die for the lies they print about us."

"I'm not a reporter," I say, "I'm only a book critic. I deal in opinions, not facts, therefore I cannot tell a lie."

"I don't give a fuck," says the sergeant, pointing his gun at me. "Join the others."

"He writes for a big London paper," continues Hannah. "His death will be front-page news."

"I don't give a shit for what the goyim think," snaps the sergeant.

"A big *Jewish* newspaper," says Hannah. The sergeant pauses.

I take my chance. "I'm better off to you alive," I say. "I'll give you my page on the paper to publicize your cause. But only if you commute our sentences."

"*Od rega*," he says, as he exits, leaving us in the care of his silent henchmen.

First comes Elijah, goes the legend, then the Messiah. So it is no surprise when Ami's sergeant returns in the company of the erstwhile Minister of Defence himself.

"It is incredible," whispers Ziz. "It is as if Abe Ratskin had returned from the dead."

"Hail the betrayer of Zion!" cries Ami.

"Where's the writer?" snaps Dom Arov. I raise my hand as if owning up to some criminal offence.

"No doubt you share your friends' opinion of me," he says, "and just as surely you would have joined them at the feet of Moses snivelling that the Egyptians had suffered enough. You make me sick, you Jews who aren't prepared to pay the price for freedom. What, you think the terrorists will go away if we say nice things to them? I had the bastards at my mercy — I was just waiting for the word to go into West Beirut and exterminate the lot. But it never came. Instead I had to tell my men: 'Stop. We must let the murderers of our children go.' Because a few of my fellow citizens got cold feet. They did not like what their **Bolshevik friends in other countries were saying about** them. They couldn't bear it, that they were not loved any more. So when those *meshugge* Phalangists massacred some Palestinians and the world said that we are the guilty ones they cried, 'Give them the head of Dom Arov!' A fine new species of Jew we have bred in this country of ours.

The goyim spread a blood libel and we apologize for it! I am kicked out of my job and the army is left kicking its heels. The whole invasion has become a farce. Put that in your paper, Mr Journalist. NOW!"

As I am about to discover, that last instruction is not addressed to me, but is actually an order to his men. Casually, languorously, they open fire upon us. Hannah, instinctively, falls upon her children. Ami falls upon her. I dive under the table with Dov Yemina and Ziz. The noise of the machine-guns is deafening, though it doesn't cover the cries of the kids.

What strikes me most about my death is the irony of it. Here, in Israel, at the hands of Jews. No need to ask what I have done to deserve it. The noseless ghost of poor Uzi stands between me and the guns, shaking his head and whispering, "Don't say you weren't warned."

He stretches out his hand as if to ease my passage, and I prepare as best I can to accept my punishment. I shut my eyes and hold my breath. The sensation, when it comes, feels like a gentle tap.

"It's all right," says Dov, his hand on my shoulder. "They're shooting blanks."

Even so, no one laughs.

"Tonight was a warning," says Dom Arov. His face is covered with drops of sweat like transparent acne. "Return to your prayers. Next time you'll need them."

And they go.

Hannah and Ami sit shaking on the floor amid the broken crockery, hugging their hysterical children. She looks up at me in utter despair, tears rolling noiselessly down her pale cheeks, and says: "Who can save us now?"

12

Not me. Nor Ziz. Nor even Dov. We leave the Valley of Tranquillity together and make our way, in my rented car, through the city toward my borrowed apartment in the German Colony. Our experience has made us unusually receptive to atmospheres and we all agree that Jerusalem seems on edge tonight, as though terrible things were happening that only daylight will reveal. How else to explain the frequent recurrence of otherwise inexplicable incidents: people running for no reason, cars speeding down empty streets. A citizen wandering through Thebes or Memphis on the eve of the Exodus probably felt much the same.

Once inside, we settle on rugs and cushions around a carved-wood coffee-table and drain a bottle filled with the distilled end-product of grain, despite the fact that it is proscribed for the next seven days.

"Is this what it's like after a battle?" I ask.

Dov laughs. "A little," he says.

"I feel as if I had just woken from a nightmare," says Ziz. "To see the man you hero-worshipped being impersonated by a monster is a shocking thing."

"It is not so strange," says Dov. "Heroism is relative. More than once during a war the unscrupulous maniac you saw tonight saved this country — because he is an unscrupulous maniac. Now he is like a shark out of water. I also am living in the wrong time. The army — my army — calls me a sentimental old fool. I tell them that they are madmen, drunk with power. Their new rule is: shoot first, ask questions later. I am sorry, but I was taught differently."

"By Wingate?" I ask.

"Among others," he says.

"Tell me about him," I say. "After all, that's why I'm here."

"The story begins at Hanita," says Dov Yemina. "Hanita was the first Jewish settlement in Western Galilee. At that time the area was banned to Jews for settlement by the White Paper the British had imposed on Palestine. But when somebody tells Jews not to do, they do.

"So the Jewish Agency decided to put up a settlement in the forbidden area and to make a power contest with the British. It was known that it would be hard to settle there and that there would be losses. The Arabs, who were at the end of their '36-'39 uprising, were very strong in this area. It was wild, there were no roads and it was very close to the Lebanese border.

"So our authorities decided to organize small groups from many kibbutzim who didn't settle yet on their own land to act as a sort of unit of the Haganah that will settle in this place. I was chosen because I knew the country and I was a veteran of the Haganah then already.

"Now most of our time we spent on night watch, patrols in the close vicinity of the place. And every three or four nights we were fired upon, either from the west — where there was a very big village, which is now a new immigrant town called Shelomi — or more often from the east — where there was a Bedouin tribe called Arab Aramshi, well known for their bravery. Within six months we had lost about ten of our group.

"One day we hear that 'the friend' is coming. Wingate wasn't called Wingate in the Haganah. He was called 'the friend'. *Hayedid* is more than friend in Hebrew, it's good friend. 'The friend' was coming to do some patrolling and to attack the marauders in their nest, which was new for us. Until that time the Haganah, even the fighting units, would usually do its fighting inside the kibbutzim, within stockades.

"As I understand, Wingate presented himself to the Jewish Agency and said that he wants to help the Yishuv and that he wants to teach the Haganah new ways of fighting. It seems that he found a common language with Yitzhak Sadeh and he was invited to Hanita to try to calm the area by going and fighting the Arabs in their bases, in their villages. Naturally I was chosen as one of those who will join him in this operation.

"In the beginning, before we started, Wingate spoke a few words of Hebrew, which was a big surprise from an English officer with the pips on and the shorts. Actually, with his very expressive features and face, he didn't look like an officer at all. From his appearance and his clothing you would say he was a scholar or something. Also he wasn't erect, you know he was always bent forward to see what's on the earth before his feet.

"Well, he led us across especially wild terrain, all covered with forest and deep wadis, as we went to attack a village of this Aramshi tribe called Jordeh, which is right on the Lebanon border, half of it was even on the other side. And this night certainly nobody can forget. First of all it was very hard, terribly hard, to cross the terrain. Then we were full of admiration for Wingate, for his know-how and for his fitness. He was very fit, though he was small and very thin. He was fit like a giant. Somehow he brought us to the place. It's a miracle, we thought, but then we learnt how to do it too.

"Coming very close to this village, which was on quite a steep hill, Wingate made a mistake, which was also maybe characteristic of the man and his motives and moral principles. He wanted to know for sure that this is Jordeh. A Bedouin passed us, coming from somewhere, very late at night, maybe two or three o'clock. So Wingate stopped him and asked in Arabic whether this is Jordeh. He said, 'Yes.' But Wingate didn't hold him up, he didn't shoot him, he let him go. And the Bedouin went away and then he ran and started to shout to the people up there, 'Beware! The Jews are coming!' Immediately they started to shoot. And what impressed me more than anything was that Wingate didn't draw back, he just told us to take cover. One of our boys, who was with the Special Night Squads for a long time, was a very good stone-thrower. So Wingate ordered him to throw a hand grenade. Then he ordered us to attack. We had no losses at all and the Bedouin ran away to Lebanon.

"Later he took us to a village on the foothill of Mount Tabor. Daburiya. And this is to be told. Because in this fighting Wingate was injured. And that's when I talked to him for a few sentences.

"It was known that there was a big gang in Daburiya and

we entered through the granary where they thresh the wheat. We came there and they met us with fire, and one of the British soldiers who had a machine-gun — the machine-gun at that time was a Lewis gun, a very heavy thing, not like the ones you saw tonight — somehow put it on a stack of wheat and started to shoot.

"Unfortunately it went down and suddenly I see that Wingate — who was a few metres from me — sits down and says, 'I was hit.' Then he got up and started to walk towards another big stack of hay. I saw that he was limping and quite badly wounded so I ran to help him and he didn't exactly hit me but he said, 'I don't need any help, I'll do it myself.' And he walked for about twenty metres and he sat under this stack and continued to give orders what and how to do.

"But that wasn't the end of it. On the following morning when we returned to our base we were in a bad mood, knowing that Wingate was hit and maybe all his plans are going to be cancelled. A few days, maybe two days, we hung about. Then, on the third day, I see him walking as if nothing has happened."

"And he rose again on the third day," says Ziz. "It reminds me of a story that's very popular in Poland at the moment."

"Wingate was no god," says Dov, "but he was no ordinary man either."

A grandfather clock that has been inconspicuously ticking in a dark corner of the room suddenly whirrs and the chimes of midnight begin.

"Still jumpy?" I ask Ziz, who is staring at the clock as if he expects Death himself to step out of its door.

"I have talked too much," says Dov. "It is time I went."

"Do you need a lift?" I ask.

"No," he says, "I like to walk."

"Is it safe?" I ask.

"If a Jew is not safe in Jerusalem," he says, "where can he be safe?"

163

"One question before you go," I say. "Do you remember . . .?" I mention the name of the man who has commissioned the book.

"Of course," says Dov. "He was with us at Hanita. We called him the Prophet, because he was always so gloomy. It turned out that he was right about our people in Europe. I heard that he died with them in one of the camps."

"No," I say, "he is still alive."

13

"Do you mind if I stay a bit longer?" asks Ziz.

"As long as you like," I say. We open a second bottle of whisky.

"I have a confession to make," says Ziz.

"Let me think," I say. "I know! You fucked my mother as well as my wife."

"This is serious," says Ziz. "Tonight, when that monster came through that door, I was sure that Abe Ratskin had come back to kill me for what I'd done to him."

"He was your hero," I say. "You worship heroes."

"Until you betray them," he says.

"So what did you do?" I say.

"Can't you guess?" he says.

"You didn't," I say.

"I did," he says. "I fucked his wife."

"Good God," I say. "Doesn't friendship mean anything to you?"

"I don't like to remind you of this, Jacob," he says, "but you have just eaten at the table of a man whose wife you had for breakfast — lunch too, so I hear."

"You sound jealous," I say, vindictively.

"Oh, Jacob," he says, "how little you know. Jealous! My friend, I have good reasons to believe that Hannah Ben-Tur is my granddaughter."

"You're joking," I say.

"I wish, I wish," he says. "Abe was away a lot — on business, as he put it — and Shaindel was a passionate woman. We had a fine time — 'Ziz, Ziz, fed on Friday, fucked on Wednesday,' she sang when I showed up for the latter — until she surprised us all by getting pregnant. It was a few weeks after one of Abe's slack periods when he was home more often than not, so it was impossible to sort out who was the baby's real father."

"If you're really her grandfather," I say, "what the hell were you doing outside her window?"

"Alas," he says, "I had no choice. She wanted me to fuck her. I couldn't tell her the truth, nor did I want her to think my refusal was on account of her mastectomy. So I told her I was impotent and got my thrills from voyeurism. Now you know why I was there and why I am so committed to Israel. I want my great-grandchildren to live in peace. Though I fear otherwise. I have read in a book that I have a namesake, a bird of monstrous proportions. This Ziz is able to protect the weaker avians from eagles and vultures by simply shrieking and flapping its wings, but at the same time a dropped feather can crush cities and a smashed egg wash away nations. You understand what I am saying?"

14

How did Shakespeare put it? "Spare your arithmetic: never count the turns; once, and a million." Hannah is more direct: "The second time is easier than the first, the third easier than the second, ad infinitum. You should be so lucky." It is Friday. We are in bed together for the fifth morning in a row. We talk about love. We talk about starting a new life together in Australia. Where's the harm? Words are like the *pontia daplicide*, here today, gone tomorrow.

It's a pleasant timetable, you'll agree. After a sandwich and a glass of beer with Hannah I take Turkish coffee in the Arab quarter with one or other of Wingate's old soldiers. Returning home, I telephone Lena. Occasionally I meet Dov or Ziz, who spends the morning at work on a poem in my quiet rooms, while I am engaged upon my own research project: the effect of spermatozoa on cancer cells.

Today, having conducted yet another experiment, we recline upon the bed listening to the radio. Since Monday night there has been a single subject for discussion: the Death Squads. We hear Dom Arov dismissing talk of a coup as nothing but rumour.

"So everything is quiet on the West Bank?" asks the interviewer.

"The people of Judaea and Samaria cannot respect a government that is in the pocket of world opinion," he says. "Nor can they trust a government that is soft on terrorism. They do not understand why I was not allowed to finish the job in Lebanon, still less why I was sacked from the cabinet. I'll tell you this, should this government of ours ever abandon the new territories as they did Sinai there will be more trouble than when the French left Algeria. *My* settlers are much nearer, and they are better armed."

We nod as Dov Yemina distinguishes between Death Squads and Special Night Squads.

"In practice there is none," he says. "In principle the SNS's were only used against our *declared* enemies. They chose their role, not us. Death Squads do not allow their victims that luxury."

"My friend is forgetting that the enemy within is the most dangerous one of all," says Dom Arov. "Surely if his wife found a lump in her breast he would not want her to commit suicide by ignoring it."

"Exactly," says a rabbi, joining the discussion. "Perhaps now we can get to the biggest problem of all: the Arabs who are living among us, who are breeding like cockroaches. Unfortunately we Jews are a merciful people so we cannot just slaughter them, though they would murder us, given the chance. They are like a cancer spreading through the body politic. Surgery is unavoidable if we are to survive. They must be cut out."

"He sounds like my surgeon," says Hannah, "with as much sense of the human cost of his proposal."

"You are still beautiful," I say. I put my hand upon that now familiar place between her thighs and let my finger pulse inside as if it were tapping out her number.

Miraculously the telephone rings in the next room.

"Shit," I say.

Hannah returns looking puzzled. "It's for you," she says. It is Lena.

"How?" I say.

"Ziz gave me the number," she says.

"Is everything OK?" I say.

"No, it isn't," she says. "You'd better come home as soon as possible. There's been an accident. Joshua's in hospital."

"Shit," I say. "Oh, God," I say. "Is it bad?" I say.

"The doctors don't know," she says. "He's unconscious."

"What happened?" I say.

"It was a lovely morning so we went for a picnic out at Kingsland Meadow," she says. "There were a few boys there. Punks or something. They called us 'Dirty Jews!' They threw stones at us. One hit Joshua on the forehead."

"Why?" I say. "In England?"

"Thanks to your friend Bruno Gascoyne," she says.

"What's he done?" I say.

"He claims we murdered his daughter," she says. She pauses. "For her blood."

"But no one believes that sort of thing any more," I say.

"Tell that to Joshua," she says.

"Oh, God," I say, "I'm going straight to the airport."

Hannah, stark naked, walks into the study. "Is something the matter?" she asks.

"Yes," I say, "I may be responsible for my son's death. Thanks to you, you deformed bitch."

15

I cannot go any faster because Ruppin Street is blocked by a procession of angry farmers marching on the Knesset.

Their leader carries a wooden cross upon which a large turkey has been crucified. From each of its pinioned wings a living bird hangs by its feet.

I think immediately of Bergner's prophetic painting, but that image fades as a more remote memory surfaces. Years ago, in my first term at grammar school, I had written a prize-winning essay on the pleasures of the countryside and been rewarded with a visit to a large farm in nearby Hertfordshire. Its owner was the brother of our red-haired science master, who consequently became my adoptive father for the day.

It was a typical afternoon in a cold, dull December, nemesis month for the farm's chief crop.

"Come, my boy," said the physics master, "let me show you one of the manifold uses of the same electricity we have been discussing in class."

He led me into a large shed made of corrugated iron, where his ruddy-faced brother and a fellow worker stood in white overalls. Just above their heads was a shining rail along which hooks were moving. Not silently. For large turkeys were suspended from them. Heads down.

As each gibbering bird passed its erstwhile benefactor he placed a metal skull-cap upon its head and passed an electric current through its brain, causing its body to twitch lasciviously until consciousness departed, whereupon the assistant snapped its neck.

"Tell this fastidious eater of kosher meat what you are doing, big brother," said my devilish guide.

"Well, son," he explained, "it's like this. If a turkey knows he's going to be killed he panics and his blood vessels burst, which discolours the flesh and makes him unsaleable. So we stun them beforehand."

Round and round they went, a never-ending carousel of death. Behind the corpses, stuck to the undulating walls, were colour photographs cut from magazines of nude women. Needless to say, I had never seen an unrelated naked breast before and found difficulty in believing that they weren't just drawings, that women were actually prepared to let strangers see their most intimate parts.

Every few moments, as I stared at the pin-ups, my view would become obscured by a turkey, a hypnotic man-oeuvre that had me imagining strange interchanges between bird and beauty. At last I understand the full meaning of that vision; those turkeys destined for the Christmas table laid down their lives in honour of the fowl now dangling before my eyes. "The Lord hear thee in the day of trouble," goes Psalm 20: "the name of the God of Jacob defend thee." His name is Turkey. I also am a turkey, being made in His likeness. Who will help us when the yeomen of England decide it is time for the harvest?

16

There is one seat left on the afternoon flight. I take it and my leave of the German Colony. Five hours later I am at Heathrow. My next stop, the hospital, is like an airport terminal, full of interior journeys, both for the mind and the body.

Joshua is in his own room in the children's ward. It is a pleasant room. Mobile butterflies dangle from the lamp-shade and dance in the light, changing partners as the heat dictates. Lena stands at the foot of the bed, watching Joshua. His favourite teddy bear is tucked up beside him.

"Is he sleeping?" I say.

"No," she says, "he's still unconscious." Unreachable.

We sit up all night, holding hands. Some time after midnight I tell Lena about Hannah Ben-Tur, carefully explaining that I only went through with it because her left breast was missing, as though my confession will magically lift the curse from Joshua.

It doesn't. He groans quietly.

"Is that a good sign?" I ask.

"What do you care?" says Lena. "You're probably not even his real father."

V Blood Libels

1

The pink-cheeked little boy who lies so relaxed upon his soft sheet of lamb's wool is like a young prince in a fairy tale, innocent victim of an evil spell, or so thinks his wicked stepfather, who blames himself and sobs for his lost son. What were my first words? "Insomnia is my inheritance, though I would have preferred amnesia." With two blows — from Lena and the stone-thrower — the genetic line has been broken; Joshua sleeps and he remembers nothing. Sometimes my heartbroken parents stand in the shadows of the dimly-lit room silently weeping. Would it help them to know that the boy may not be their grandson at all?

My wife, their daughter-in-law, is now a stranger. We sleep in the wards on alternate nights, and ask only after Joshua's well-being. What follows is an accurate record of our last conversation:

"What do you care? You're probably not even his real father."

"Impossible. We were in love. There was no one else."

"You fool! Why do you think you got the job on the *Jewish Voice*?"

"Tit for tat. I see. Does the editor know?"

"What?"

"That he might be Joshua's father?"

"Of course not."

There is no doubt that Lena wanted to torture me as she spoke. But until that moment I really believe she had all but forgotten the first of her marital infidelities and never gave a thought to Joshua's paternity.

Despite the fact that she is — or was — a teacher of history she has no eye for the double-exposure that occurs when the past surreptitiously superimposes itself upon the present. Her memories are like holiday snaps, stored innocuously beneath the bed. She, who participated, never thinks of Uzi or Ziz while I, who can only imagine, am reminded of them a dozen times a day. It is a curse which Joshua has been spared.

And yet the doctors can find nothing wrong with him; according to them he should have woken up by now. I have stood beside a light-box with consultants in some obscure part of the hospital and been shown X-rays of his skull which confirm there are no fractures, neither hairline nor — God forbid — depressed.

In one of our passionate encounters Hannah named my parts from head to toe. The Hebrew for skull, I recall, is *goolgolet*, hence the hill called Golgotha. Nor was it a coincidence that Joshua received his wound on Easter. Certainly his skull resembles a hill such as Silbury, likewise full of secret chambers. There suspended within is the unreachable brain, unharmed according to the scans, but isolated, independent of its progenitors; head of a body that is not tyrannized by its organs. On the contrary, they are hardly required.

Presently Joshua is fed by an intravenous drip and cleaned out by naso-gastric tubes and catheters. Machines are also readily available to replace the kidneys and lungs if required. At night the only sounds in the darkened room are the throbbing of pumps and Joshua's regular breathing.

As I have said, I cannot sleep. So I count the months as if they were sheep. But the answer always comes out the same. Joshua was born in November 1980. I began work at the *Jewish Voice* nine months earlier. Either of us could be his father. Lena would undoubtedly say, "What difference does it make? You love him, he doesn't." But it is not enough. I need proof. So how are questions of paternity resolved? With blood, of course! As I recall, the child must belong to the same group as one of his parents: A plus B cannot produce O. Counterfeiting slumber, I watch the nurse as she pays her midnight call, checking Joshua's vital signs, changing the green or yellow bottles, and swabbing his back and buttocks with surgical spirit to prevent sores. When she has gone, I examine the bulletin board at the foot of the bed, where all the test results are recorded, and discover the mineral components of his blood, but not its type.

"Excuse me," I say to the registrar in his open white coat and old school tie as he makes his rounds, "but do you happen to know my son's blood type?"

"I've got it somewhere, old chap," he says. "Can't it wait?"

"Not really," I say. "You see, I faint at the sight of blood. So does my wife. But we've decided to become donors. Or one of us has. The one whose blood matches Joshua's. It's our way of saying 'thank you'."

"A nice gesture, old chap," he says, reading the case notes. "Your boy is A-Neg. Good news for you, I hope."

OK, so I've taken the first step; should my blood group not be A-Negative the editor will be able to claim a new addition to his family. If it is A-Negative, then I'm still in with a chance, though so is the editor if he is also A-Negative. Heaven knows how I'll obtain that information. Besides, I still don't know my own group.

2

Having lied about donating the stuff, it occurs to me that it might be the easiest way of defining my particular type, notwithstanding my genuine prejudice against the sight of blood, especially my own. I do not tell Lena my intentions, nor anyone at the *Jewish Voice*, from where I take a taxi to the National Blood Transfusion Service at London Wall.

To enter the building it is necessary to ascend a high walkway and pass office suppliers and wine merchants until you come to an incongruous plate-glass window that lists the good deeds your blood is capable of performing once it is separated from your body, that ill-fated accommodation.

The environment, which consists entirely of modern towers, conspires to reinforce those intimations of insignificance. Within the offices are thousands of souls, each with their own aspirations. And you think: *What makes me so special?*

Surely the posters in the window are right; only when stripped of their individuality could my blood and organs make amends for all the misfortune that I have accidentally caused *in propria persona*. Should I not grant them their triumph this instant and plunge to the pavement below? *Jump*, cry my kidneys. *Chicken shit*, hisses my liver, as I enter the building instead. Turning left, I see a nurse who beckons me to a seat and, without bothering to introduce herself, proceeds to ask me the most intimate questions about my recent history. Have I ever had hepatitis? Scarlet fever? Syphilis? Measles? Do I take drugs? When did I last have a cold? She notes my answers on a card.

Behind her is a large filing-cabinet presided over by an upright gentleman whose own curriculum vitae must include a spell in the military. Once, no doubt, he assured his men that there was no nobler deed than to shed one's blood for one's country. Now, having dispensed with those messy preliminaries, he has at his fingertips an army of blood, robust red corpuscles in their billions, just waiting for the order to go forth and vanquish the enemy.

I, too, am ready to pay the price. I raise the forefinger on my left hand, and look away quickly as the nurse removes a sterilized razor blade from a wallet and nicks me just above the cuticle. Throwing the blade away, she squeezes the fingertip, collects the bloody beads on a glass rod, and deposits them in test-tubes.

"Is that enough to establish my blood type?" I ask.

"Oh, yes," she says. "We'll tell you afterwards."

"Not before?" I ask.

"Oh, no," she says.

So I'll have to go through with it! Perhaps the blood sacrifice will redeem my son, as the ejaculation of sperm into a foreign receptacle surely condemned him.

Thus it is with some hope that I fill in the requisite forms, collect my plastic bag, and lie myself down upon an empty bed still warm from its previous occupier.

Blood Libels

"Are you Jacob Silkstone?" asks a new nurse.

"I am," I reply.

My reward is a needle thrust into my arm. Needing no further prompting, my blood runs joyfully along the plastic tube and begins to fill the bag which the nurse has fixed to a stand on the floor.

"Is this your first time?" she asks.

I nod.

"It's best not to watch," she says. "I'll come back soon to check everything's going all right. In the meantime, pump on this."

She places a wooden dowel the size of a pencil in my hand. "It keeps the flow regular," she says.

Press on, press on, whispers my liver, until all is red. Red the dawn! Red the revolution! Red the future!"

See, say my lungs, see how easy it is. Why don't you let us all go? Think how much good we could do. Yes, you must die that others may live. You must die.

I am becoming weaker, but my resolve is strengthening. As I pump with growing abandon the dowel grows until it stretches from hand to hand behind my back. Then a trunk emerges from an invisible knot at its centre and, as it lengthens, it swivels to an upright position, leaving me hanging on to the crossbeam for dear life. Pity me in my passion as my life-blood drains away. Forgive my son, for he knew not what I did.

After they have cut me down and led me to the recovery room, they give me a glass of orange juice and a handful of iron tablets and as I leave they present me with an offical-looking document, proof of my heroism.

Walking down the street I read the details on the certificate. Glory hallelujah! I'm A-Neg too! Positive reinforcement, but not definite proof. If only I could persuade the editor to do likewise.

174

3

"You look pale," says the editor's secretary.

I explain that I have been elsewhere, performing a *mitzvah*. "Couldn't you convince him to follow my example?" I say, nodding towards the editor's office. "Think how good it would be for the Jews at this difficult time if our big-wigs were seen lining up outside the Transfusion Centre."

"Tell him yourself," she says. "He wants to see you."

"Your protégé is on telly tonight," says the editor. "Watch him, please, and phone in four hundred words before ten-thirty. By the way, how's the kid? Any change?"

Why does he want to know? What business is it of his?

Reclining on the sofa in the permanent twilight of Joshua's hospital room I turn on the television. Bruno Gascoyne's unsubstantiated claim that his daughter had been slaughtered in some secret Semitic ritual, the immediate cause of Joshua's present condition, has excited dubious academic interest in the obscure ends of such juvenile martyrs as William of Norwich and Hugh of Lincoln. Hence the edition of *Panorama* devoted to the subject, the climax of which goes like this:

> INTERVIEWER: Mr Gascoyne, surely you don't expect us to swallow these disgraceful accusations against the Jews?
> GASCOYNE: I merely ask that you listen to my words. If any are going to be eaten I have no doubt that they will be your own.
> INTERVIEWER: I'm all ears.
> GASCOYNE: Very well. It is a fact that there were numerous unholy murders of Christian children in twelfth- and thirteenth-century England, at least a dozen of which have been fully authenticated. The bodies of these poor innocents, so the records tell us, bore the unmistakable marks of ritual slaughter and forcible circumcision. It is also true that these

killings ended with the expulsion of the Jews. Perhaps it is just a coincidence, but I am old-fashioned enough to believe that there is no smoke without fire.

INTERVIEWER: But that was seven hundred years ago. Why drag it up today?

GASCOYNE: I'll show you.

So saying, Bruno Gascoyne holds up a large photograph which the cameras reprint on five million television screens simultaneously. It shows the abandoned and naked corpse of his daughter hanging upside down from a large oak tree in Kingsland Meadow, a cord tied around one ankle.

INTERVIEWER: That's enough.

GASCOYNE: No, no. I want everyone to look carefully at her throat. Do you see that it has been cut? No doubt by a shocket who learned his craft on cows. I am told that the Jews stood beneath her bleeding body with their silver bowls held out.

INTERVIEWER: Why haven't you told all this to the police?

GASCOYNE: Think. Picture our Home Secretary. Do you seriously believe that he would permit enquiries into my accusations? Of course not. He will protect his own. As we must. All I can hope is for the indigenous people of England to spit upon these Jewish bloodsuckers and profiteers who have drained our country dry. Let them rise up as they did in the days of Edward I and expel the aliens from our blessed shores. Otherwise as my daughter is today, so their children will be tomorrow.

INTERVIEWER: I now call upon Rabbi Joseph Nathan, a member of the Board of Deputies of British Jews, to refute these slanders, for which I apologize.

RABBI NATHAN: First I must say how shocked I am at the BBC for permitting the broadcast of such foul libels, the likes of which have not been heard since the days of Goebbels and Streicher.

GASCOYNE: You are a hypocrite, sir, as well as being a windbag.

INTERVIEWER: Please!

GASCOYNE: Can Rabbi Nathan deny that on 21 May 1961 in the ladies' lavatories of the Café Royal he forced the act of fellatio upon the unwilling person of Helga M, then the German au pair of the *Jewish Voice*'s present literary editor?

RABBI NATHAN: This is scandalous!

GASCOYNE: It is all here.

And he raises aloft in triumph a copy of that rare book, *Rabbi Nathan's Folly*.

RABBI NATHAN: I'll sue for libel.

GASCOYNE: You do that. But the truth will out, in the words of our first great poet. With Rabbi Nathan's permission I should like to quote a relevant passage from the *Canterbury Tales*, unless he wants Chaucer gagged too.

RABBI NATHAN: Go ahead.

GASCOYNE: "Our firste fo, the serpent Sathanas,
    That hath in Jewes herte his waspes nest,
    Up swal, and seide, 'O Hebraik peple, allas!
    Is this to yow a thing that is honest,
    That swich a boy shal walken as him lest
    In your despyt, and singe of swich sentence,
    Which is agayn your lawes reverence?'
    Fro thennes forth the Jewes han conspyred
    This innocent out of this world to chace;
    An homicyde ther-to han they hyred,
    That in an aley hadde a privee place;
    And as the child gan for-by to pace,
    This cursed Jew him hente and heeld him
        faste,
    And kitte his throte, and in a pit him caste.

177

Blood Libels
I seye that in a wardrobe they him threwe
Wher-as these Jewes purgen hir entraille.
O cursed folk of Herodes al newe,
What may your yvel entente yow availle?
Mordre wol out, certain, it wol nat faille,
And namely ther th'onour of God shal
    sprede,
The blood out cryeth on your cursed dede."
Does the rabbi — not an expert on *English* literature,
I suspect — want to tell the British people that not
only Chaucer but also Shakespeare, Marlowe and
Dickens are liars? Does he want to sue them too?
RABBI NATHAN: Literature is not life!
GASCOYNE: So *Rabbi Nathan's Folly* is not the
truth?

The programme ends in uproar. But it is an ill wind, as
they say, since my long-suffering agent is able to auction
off the paperback rights for a small fortune the following
morning. Suddenly I am rich enough to quit my job, a man
of independent means, a voice in the land.

4

That same day the offices of the *Jewish Voice* are besieged
by members of the British Party carrying banners which
call us "Christ Killers" and "Bloodsuckers". Inside, the
editor calls me a quisling and fires me before I have a
chance to resign.
"If I could cut off your hand, I would," he adds.
His action is not without a certain poetry, for the life
expectancy of the *Jewish Voice*, assuming that it is not torn
up, burned or otherwise disposed of, is approximately
thirty-five years. This means that the issue which carried
my birth announcement, a document of some importance I
have never bothered to verify, is about to enter the last
stages of terminal jaundice somewhere in the attic of my
parents' house. Meanwhile Mr and Mrs Silkstone themselves are doubtless cowering in the cellar, so as not to hear

Rabbi Nathan's call, and cursing the day their son was born.

And who can blame them? Not me, certainly. It cannot be pleasant suddenly to become a pariah in the suburb where you have dwelt among neighbours for nearly forty years. In rapid succession I have betrayed wife, son and parents, all of whom no longer recognize me. But am I really that guilty? Was fucking beautiful, sick Hannah Ben-Tur such a crime? Was writing *Rabbi Nathan's Folly* a capital offence? God knows how Bruno Gascoyne got hold of a copy. But now the world knows of it, why should I not claim authorship? Lena might be able to take Joshua away from me, but even she cannot deny that I wrote the book her father printed. It is all that I have left: my talent.

We have been advised by the Special Branch not to leave the building in groups of less than three. Being one of the last to go, I am invited, despite my status as excommunicant, to accompany the editor and his secretary on the dangerous walk to the station.

As we enter the street a crop-haired youth with an embryonic face bares his throat and dares us to cut it.

"No, thanks," I say, "you're too anaemic. *Shvartzer* blood is healthier. You can make wholemeal matzohs out of it."

"Oh, don't make a joke like that," whispers the editor's secretary, "not even in jest." Words of wisdom, as it turns out. For sticks and stones begin to rain upon us.

"You and your tongue . . . " begins the editor, as we start our run to the main road. But he fails to complete the curse. A lump of granite strikes him on the back of the head and he half-turns as if to upbraid his attacker. Instead he receives a blow from a fence post full in the face and drops as if pole-axed.

"Oh, God!" screams his secretary. "They've murdered him!"

"Dead men don't groan," I say. "Go and get an ambulance. I'll stay here."

The crusaders, having taken their revenge, are no longer

around to hinder her. When she has gone I kneel beside my ex-editor and observe that his cheek has been split wide open so that I can see his immaculate tongue fluttering within amid bubbles of blood. I know enough to make a pillow out of my jacket and place it beneath his good cheek, thereby ensuring that he will not drown in his own gore. Having made my semi-conscious cuckolder, potential father of my cuckoo, as comfortable as possible, I collect his blood as it dribbles off his prickly chin into my empty hip-flask. It is not a reliquary, more a means of transport. For I intend to take the contents, while still fresh, to the Blood Transfusion Centre where, if need be, I will bribe a nurse to satisfy my curiosity.

5

I get no further than St Paul's. There, amid the vandalized trees, I disturb a scavenging magpie which screeches and rises from the ground, its white scapulars shining like newly won stripes, its long green and purple tail gleaming like an oil slick. This, in turn, arouses a terrestrial denizen of the graveyard, his loves and hates stippled upon his muscular arms, who stops me in my tracks.

"Hey!" he shouts to some neighbouring troglodytes, "I've caught a Jewboy on the hop. Let's have some fun."

Within moments, six of the subhumans in their variously soiled sweat-shirts are prodding me with their grubby fingers as if I were the freak. "Your wallet," says their leader. "Give."

I give. A robbery I can handle, if that's what this is.

"Fucking plastic," he says, flicking through the credit cards. "Where's the money, Jewboy?" The prods become stabs as the fingernails bite into my flesh, which is already anticipating its martyrdom.

But then, miraculously, Lena wins me a reprieve. "Hep! Hep!" shouts the skin-headed führer. "Take a butchers at Madam Silkstone." And he holds up a photograph of Lena supine upon a sunbed, her private parts now public property. "Just look at the bush on that Jewess," he says. "I bet the bitch has a cunt to match. Do you think she'd like half a dozen pork sausages, Jewboy? All at once."

"Listen," I say, "if you let me go I'll tell you where you can find her."

"You'll do better than that, mister," says my captor, "you'll show us."

"If you insist," I say.

"You're too compliant," he says, "even for a Jew. You must be hiding something. Let's search the fucker." Thus they find the hip-flask, my only other possession.

I watch with a hopeless fascination close to masochistic pleasure as their chief unscrews the top and throws his head back to take a gulp. It springs forward immediately, revealing the lips of a vampire.

"The fucking thing's full of blood," he yelps, stating the obvious.

"Whose blood?" they wonder.

"A good question," they agree.

"Wait a minute," says a malign dwarf wrapped up in a Union Jack. "Remember what Badger said. I bet this fucking yid has murdered one of our kids. He's a child killer and we've got the blood to prove it."

Suddenly these former outlaws are transformed into law-abiding citizens of the Commonwealth, intent upon protecting their time-honoured civilization from alien practices such as infanticide. Casting aside such parochial pursuits as mass rape, they drag their pathetic catch along the very streets he had planned to take until they reach the aptly named Barbican Police Station.

The desk sergeant looks up but his face registers no surprise, the fixed expression of world-weariness being a necessary part of his uniform, a device to demonstrate impartiality. No, clues to his real feelings must be sought in the objects he has placed upon his desk: a St Christopher medallion, a thriller by Dornford Yates and a scandal sheet which screams in 100pt Souvenir Bold, "Another Kid Missing." More ominous is the question it poses: "Is there a connection?" I am outvoted 7-1 on that point and escorted to a cell, a suspected member of the bloody conspiracy.

"This is not Tsarist Russia," I comfort myself, "nor am I Mendel Beilis." *Now you know how we feel, says my liver, in a mocking tone, and we're lifers, not overnight guests like yourself.*

I thank God for the decree of habeas corpus. Tomorrow I will be free unless, by some perverse coincidence, the editor's blood matches that of any unclaimed child in the local morgue.

But tomorrow, as insomniacs well know, can sometimes seem a too-distant dream, an intangible brightness that fails to illuminate the gloomy here and now. Filled with primitive fears, I curl up in the corner of my prison like an unborn foetus condemned by cowardice to caesarean birth.

The night seems endless but, strange thing, the longer I go without seeing the blinding flash of scalpel light the happier I become. For the first time since I turned eleven I am free of responsibility. I have become an irrelevancy. I am safe. The feeling does not last — how could it?

Footfalls in the corridor and the pecuniary sound of keys on a chain remind me that the likely corollary to my new-found emotional security is physical danger. The door opens.

"Follow me," says the sergeant. "I want you to see something."

In an elevator we ascend to the top of a dark tower and look down upon a dynamic swarm of demonstrators swirling in and out of the streets, all drunk upon righteous anger, beer and rhetoric. The last belonging to Bruno Gascoyne, who stands on the back of an open lorry gesticulating like an Elizabethan orator, the white streak in his thick hair flashing like a fluorescent beacon beneath the neon street lamps.

Growing younger with every minute, Gascoyne nimbly leaps upon the roof of the van, where he stands, arms outstretched, shouting: "Follow me!" And as the lorry moves slowly down the road it draws the crowds as though in obedience to some seldom-heard call of nature, the spitting oriflamme of their firebrands a hot replica of the cold stars and quasars that pulsate in the sky above.

"They're heading north," says the sergeant.

6

The ancients believed that influenza was caused by the malign influence of the stars, hence its name. The rational Victorians, on balance, felt that some morbific principle was probably present in the atmosphere during an epidemic, but were unable to determine the nature of the infecting agent until 1892, when Richard Pfeiffer isolated an ill-intentioned bacillus, *hemophilus influenzae*, a runty organism which cannot prosper without blood, not unlike those efficiently organized specks, sons and daughters of the crowds who once came to Wingate Football Club to taunt us, disappearing up Goshawk Road.

It is now known that the primary cause of influenza is an alphabetical virus which gains entry through the mouth or the nose and selectively attacks and destroys the cells lining the respiratory tract.

Once again a prisoner in my own inhospitable cell, I begin to empathize with the nuclei at the centre of those other beleagured cells. They are superficially situated and not intimately bathed in the fluids of the bloodstream, relying for protection upon their own physiological mechanisms. But once the cells are damaged, all the benign fluid from the blood is lost and inflammation takes hold of the supporting tissue.

Thereafter, with the antibodies on the run, the invading virus attacks the body politic itself. As if in sympathy, I begin to burn one minute and shiver the next. When I feel hot, the walls are cool, but when I am cold the walls scorch my hands. A band of heated iron tightens around my forehead, like renegade tanks surrounding the seat of government, the pressure of which descends to my feet causing every muscle en *route* to ache.

Gradually the chills abate and I am left in a state of constant fever. Sweat springs from my open pores, filling the cell with a singularly musty odour, not unlike the earthy smell that permeates the cellar in my parents' house. What strength I possessed drains from my body, leaving me with a remarkable depression of spirits, a despondency based upon an unutterable premonition. The stars are indeed malign tonight, I fear.

By morning I am on the edge of delirium and it hardly registers when I am released for lack of evidence. The editor's blood, it seems, does not match any known corpse still available. Unfortunately I forget to ask for the return of my precious sample, though I can hardly remember what I wanted it for in the first place.

I do notice, however, that the air smells lightly charred, as if Nature were arranging its own funeral games, though it could just as easily be the internal cause of the strange aroma my skin has been exhaling. In short, I am very confused. Am I still in the cell, or am I in my car, or am I floating through my own bloodstream?

Dead cells swirl by, or are they specks of charcoal rushing along the torrential gutters? Who are the grey shadows flittering among the smouldering ruins? Fugitives or firemen? Everywhere I look there are lines of men; some pass tongues of flame from hand to hand, others buckets of water.

"Silkstone," orders my science master, "come and hold this ball." It is attached by a chain to Gravesand's Ring, which it fits exactly, except when hot. It is red hot. "Scared, are we, Silkstone?"

Yes, but I'll do it. Not then, but now.

Now my flesh is on fire. And in my feverish vision I see the Children of Albion violate the privacy of suburban privet hedges, exposing brilliant green lawns and expansive houses. As my temperature rises, the sprinklers begin to spin webs of sweat which soon turn to steam in the vicious heat.

Blood Libels

I see my devilish kidneys distributing the *Protocols of the Elders of Zion,* and my Bolshie liver haranguing the masses, making their blood boil.

Through the humid smoke pass the Children of Albion, pledged to avenge the deaths of innocent martyrs, and in their righteous anger they drive the secretive strangers from their safe homes with hoes and rakes.

And yet it is me my co-religionists scream at, as if I were the Angel of Death passing among them, making a mockery of every device they have constructed to ward him off: hedges, burglar alarms, mezuzoth, windows, curtains, doors, material possessions, telephones, medicines, incantations are all useless when the incurable moment eventually arrives.

The men and boys are butchered on the spot with spades and saws and hammers and knives and axes, while mothers and daughters are stripped of their clothes and made to crawl across gory grass so that they seem in my delirious gaze like a pure white herd of grazing cows, pissing and shitting as such animals do.

By way of recreation, the Children of Albion play soccer with severed heads, using naked women on all fours as living goalposts, some of whom faint as they recognize a face that rolls beneath the belly that gave it life.

Those who remain on their knees are taken from behind by both winners and losers, so that their flanks stiffen and their teats shudder. Or else their mouths are forced.

Nor is that the end of their suffering, for they have yet to be raped with spotless milk bottles the Children of Albion have gathered from doorsteps and refrigerators. When emptied, these are refilled with gasoline, stoppered with rags, lit, then thrown at the windows of the houses, whereupon traitorous curtains leap for joy and it rains splinters of glass.

Terrified birds, canaries, budgerigars, even macaws, hoopoes and cockatoos escape through the shattered panes, their wings aflame, only to crash to the ground, as if shot down by gravity, in a stink of overdone plumage. The few survivors are brought to earth by well-flighted catapults.

Cats and dogs of every breed run amok until most are kebabed upon garden forks. Some, however, defect to the enemy and are rewarded with permission to lap up the unholy brew of milk and semen dribbling from the swollen lips of their former guardians.

Videos, stereos, radios, televisions, cameras, clocks, lamps, vases, mirrors and photographs are dragged from the burning houses and smashed to pieces in an insane vengeance upon anything that may once have pleasured the senses of their owners. Cars, too, are ignited; and all are left like crashed sky-chariots, plumes of foul-smelling black smoke marking their fatal descent.

Thus the advance guard clears the way for Bruno Gascoyne himself, who appears riding bareback upon a unicorn, a scythe at his shoulder. Slowly, triumphantly, he weaves among the debris and corpses, pausing at any that still show signs of life to administer the *coup de grâce* with his mount's pearly horn.

Pigs make up the rearguard. These are left alone to rut greedily among the bodies, assisted only by gourmand-izing hedgehogs. Is this hell? No, it is Hendon. Is that Rabbi Nathan intoning the prayers for the dead? Or is it my heart? Will I die when he stops beating his chest? Are those my parents wringing their hands? Above us all, with the answers, hovers the Angel of Death, a burnished figure that shimmers in the glow of the burning suburb. His helmet is silver, his body is glass, mercury fills his veins.

7

For three more nights my fever rages. On the fourth morn-ing I awake to a new world. Astral-tripping and ethereal whispering reveal that Golders Green and Hendon have been set alight by Gascoyne's anti-Semitic storm-troopers; forty Jews have been murdered, another five hundred injured. Ten synagogues have been destroyed as well as two hundred houses. From Golders Green and Hendon the disturbances spread north, south, east and west; nor are they yet at an end.

My parents' house was ransacked, but they were spared, being hidden in the cellar, as I had envisioned. Lena is also safe, so far as I know, having taken refuge in the hospital where Joshua slept through the whole disturbance, where he still sleeps on. I do not blame her for not enquiring after my welfare. We lived in different times. Firmly rooted in the present she looked toward the future, while I clung to the past, wherein everything is already known. I realize now that I was never really present for her and that when she said "I can see right through you" she meant it literally. I was as transparent as the homunculus that has spooked my life, more interested in my bodily functions than her emotional needs. My organs have their triumph, their malfeasance has brought my story to a close. I am trapped, overthrown.

As if the pogroms in England were his cue, Dom Arov finally seizes power in Israel, with extraordinary ease; no one, it seems, has the will to stop him. A few weeks after the event I receive a letter from Israel. "My dear Jacob," it begins, "perhaps you will be surprised that I and not Hannah am writing to you. But I have some news that I hope will not shock you too greatly. Hannah, my beloved wife, is dead. Dead at thirty-five. The doctors were wrong. The cancer had spread further than they thought. Its advance was rapid. Shockingly so. I will spare you the details. Perhaps, after Arov's putsch, she no longer wanted to live. I cannot blame her. What is happening is not pleasant. Dov Yemina was picked up by a Death Squad here, in Jerusalem, and has not been heard of since. My turn will come. Of that I have no doubt. Indeed, I no longer care for myself. But, O my friend, what will become of our children?"

8

No doubt, in years to come, when historians begin to write objectively about the destruction of Anglo-Jewry they will delineate the "remote origins" and "immediate causes" without ever mentioning the events I have outlined in these pages. They will describe the mass unemployment and lawlessness ascribed by Gascoyne to Jewish politicians and how in the wake of the first pogroms a weak Prime Minister accepted the resignation of his Chancellor and Home Secretary for being too intellectual and out of touch with the fears of ordinary people, thereby seeming to withdraw government protection from us, but I beg you to believe me when I say how wrong they will be. For history is not some pseudo-scientific study of facts, best pursued when the protagonists are securely posthumous. It does not march forward in an orderly line, nor even dialectically, like a knight on a chess board.

No, permit me to introduce the psychosomatic approach to history. Just as the mind, knowing the symptoms, has no need of bacillus or virus to counterfeit an illness, so history does not need facts to proceed. What people believe to have happened is more important than what actually did. Without a shred of evidence Gascoyne has persuaded the British to accept the ancient libels and forced the government to set up a Commission of Inquiry. In the meantime his followers continue to kill Jews with impunity, convinced they are purging the body politic. My own body, I may add, is still plagued by the flu virus, against which it seems to have no resistance.

Paul Klee wrote, "To stand despite all possibilities to fall." Well, I have given up the struggle and surrendered to gravity. Here I am curled up in my former bed in my old bedroom, passively resisting my liver and its rumours. Every day being Yom Kippur I don't sleep, I don't eat and I don't shit except when my distraught parents overpower me (not a great feat) and force a suppository into me. Oh, Dom Arov swears vengeance upon our murderers, while

killing as many Jews himself, and the hero of Kingsland
Meadow knowingly invokes the ghost of Wingate. Even
my father kicks a football around, hoping to form a team,
despite the admonitions of my open-eyed mother.

"You are an optimistic fool!" she cries.

And she is right. There is no cure for what ails me. Not
now. Perhaps when Joshua, *kayn aynhoreh*, awakens from
his dreamless sleep.

My own diurnal visions exceed my worst nightmares, as
though my subconscious had suddenly populated the
world. Not that my world is very large. On the contrary, it
has shrunk to the size of a room, which is where I came in,
of course. Like the baby I formerly was, I am once again
over-dependent upon my parents, who are forced to nurse
me through my dreadful malaise, though they are not out
of the woods themselves. There is, I realize, only one place
where we can all be safe. Wingate Football Club. I beg my
father to take us all, including my mother.

"You're crazy," he says. "It's finished. They closed
down the ground last year to build a motorway."

My best hope — gone!

How can I convey to you the joy — yes, joy! — of
attending Wingate Football Club? Picture a boy — barely
older than Joshua — walking hand in hand with his father
down a path of granite chips which opens out upon a
brilliant green field, close-cropped and subdivided by
dazzling white lines. Already present will be two hundred
or so loyal supporters — all Jews — every one of whom
knows our names. There's the Prince of Shmattes, of
course, and Mickey Rose the jeweller, who made me a
double-headed penny and gave rise to my first joke:
"Mickey Rose sat on a pin. Mickey Rose." And there's
half-blind Bernie Rothstein, who emigrated to South
Africa, and his wife, Miriam, who sold the glossy
programmes and raffle tickets for a shilling each. Always
she said, "You'll win this week, Jakie." But all I cared
about was the team, displayed in the centre-spread like a
pyramid, and whether my particular hero, Mose Tapper,

was playing on the right wing. They were my heroes, the men of Wingate Football Club, as they trotted on to the pitch in their blue and white strip, the Star of David emblazoned on their hearts.

Railway lines leading from London to Scotland ran along an embankment behind the stadium and the drivers of the old steam locomotives often slowed down to watch the play and wave while the smokestacks on their engines sent signals into the sky. For years I believed that the rainclouds which mysteriously marred cerulean skies began their careers in those boilers, a theory not reached without empirical evidence. Many times I observed an innocent head of steam rise and grow until it covered the heavens. Everything gone, all lost, as ephemeral as smoke!

"You must bear witness," I tell my father, "record the history of Wingate Football Club before all our names are forgotten."

For days thereafter my father shuts himself in his bedroom and, through the thin wall that separates us, I hear my first typewriter reactivated. Eventually, unable to restrain my curiosity any longer, I arise from my bed for the first time since the onset of my illness and shakily enter the room where my story began.

It is a rare sight that greets me, both parents asleep. The floor is littered with discarded drafts, none of which bear any resemblance to the expected chronicle. Instead of salvaging our identities from the wreckage of the present my father has been wasting his time over a letter to my wife!

> Dear Lena,
> I know you have enough problems of your own. Indeed, there is not a moment that goes by when we are not thinking of little Joshua and praying for him. God forbid we should burden you with more trouble, but we do not know what to do about Jakie. To be frank, Lena, his behaviour is killing us. Believe me, it is no pleasure administering

suppositories to a man in his thirties. But he will not purge himself. Nor will he eat. All he talks about are pogroms in his belly and the need to starve his enemies, though our doctor swears there is nothing wrong with him. Nothing physical, anyway.

Lena, we can't take much more, and there is no one else we can turn to. You are still his wife, after all, and still have some responsibilities. Forgive me! But I must tell you a secret we have kept from everyone, including Jakie, for 35 years. He is adopted. Until now we have always loved him as if he were our own son, but enough is enough. If Rabbi Nathan hadn't made such a big deal in the synagogue about his birth we wouldn't have had to keep so quiet about it. But after that, how could we tell everyone that Jakie wasn't even Jewish? I may not know who his parents were, but of that I am certain: there isn't a drop of Jewish blood in him. It seemed a harmless enough deception but it must have been very wrong. Why else are we being punished?

"It's a lie!" I scream. "A bloody lie!"
But mine is a voice in the wilderness.